DREAM GIRL

S. J. LOMAS

Monroe County Library,
Thanks for the
support. Keep up
the great work!

S. J. Lomas
2015

Dream Girl

Published by Scribe Publishing Company
Royal Oak, Michigan
www.scribe-publishing.com

All rights reserved.

Copyright © 2013 by S.J. Lomas

ISBN 978-0-9859562-9-5

Printed in the U.S.

DEDICATION

To Jeff, Patty and Ted
Because, I love you most of all.

1

Christine

My mom was the first to crack. Standing under the domestic departures sign at Detroit Metro Airport, she clutched the handle of her carry-on bag as tears filled her eyes.

"You're a young woman," she sniffed. "Perfectly capable of taking care of yourself this summer." I don't know which of us she was trying to reassure.

I looked down, not strong enough to face my own mother's tears.

Suddenly, she crushed me close in an embrace that practically knocked the wind out of me.

"It's all going to be fine, sweetheart," she cried. "Don't you worry about a thing."

"Mom," I mumbled into her shoulder. "Don't miss your flight. Don't you and Dad have an appointment right away, or something?"

I felt her nodding.

"Yes," she sniffed. "Carpet for the new house. Any requests?"

"Whatever. It's not my house."

Mom pushed me to arm's length to look at me.

Tears were actually falling down her cheeks now and I instantly regretted what I'd said. We'd all been hoping my dad would get a huge promotion, but none of us expected it'd come with a transfer to Texas.

I shrugged. "Blue, maybe?"

Mom bit her lip and nodded again. "Blue carpet sounds lovely."

"Yeah," I said, bouncing the rubber toe of my shoe against the curb.

"I love you, Christine. Have fun at Daria's, okay?"

"I will. Love you, too."

Mom hesitated for a second like maybe she wasn't really going to go. Like maybe it had all been an elaborate prank that had gone on too long. But a light came into her eyes, and she slipped her hand into the back pocket of her bag and pulled a small package out.

"I almost forgot," she said. "This is for you."

I took it from her and unwrapped a hardcover copy of *Jane Eyre,* my favorite book. I'd been wanting a nice copy of it, not just a cheap paperback that would yellow and crumble apart in a couple years.

"Wow, Mom. Thanks!" I said, running my finger over the cool gold-edged pages, loving the perfect smoothness.

Mom managed a small smile, even as a fresh spring of tears began to flow. She turned and walked into the terminal without looking back.

I exhaled slowly and climbed into the car with my beautiful new book. As I pulled away from the curb, all I could think was that I only had eleven weeks to figure out how to stay in Michigan.

2

Christine

Fifteen minutes late for work, I hurried through the employee entrance at the public library and ditched my purse in my locker. Sucking in a deep breath, I scurried past the row of supervisor offices on my right. I escaped detection in supervisor alley, and made it to the staff copy room, where our mailboxes resided. As soon as I scooted in to retrieve my nametag, I discovered my boss, Laura Fawcett, talking to a guy who wore his brown t-shirt and carpenter jeans really well. At least, he looked good from behind, which was all I could see of him.

I tried to inconspicuously snake my arm around them to access my mailbox, but Laura stopped me.

"Christine," she said. "I'd like you to meet Gabriel, our new page."

"Hi," Gabriel said as he turned toward me.

I should have tossed out a welcoming smile and a "Nice to meet you. Gotta run," but the strong outline of his back did nothing to prepare me for the siren song of his front. Melancholy practically poured off him, nearly visible, yet transient as smoke. His tousled brown hair, square-ish face, Johnny Depp lips and intense brown eyes nearly knocked me backwards. In that brief instant of eye contact, I felt the disorienting fuzziness that comes between sleep and wakefulness. Tiny flecks of autumn amber sparkled in his eyes, beckoning me deeper. My lips parted, as if not under my control, and prepared to utter some sort of greeting but stopped. I noticed the slightest twinge in my brain.

Strange but not unpleasant, it felt like a warm breeze had just blown away a cobweb from my mind. Jarred by all these things happening in an instant, I turned away. Even so, I could feel his eyes on me as I fled. It made the entire length of my spine tingle.

Mentally kicking myself for behaving like an idiot in front of a hot new guy, I shook off the residual feeling of ants crawling over my back and focused on the task at hand: exemplary customer service. A long line snaked from the check out desk. I quickly assumed my post, right between my friends, Tiffany and Daria, turned the sign from closed to open and looked up with my public service smile. "I can help the next person in line," I trilled.

When a lull finally came, Daria was the first to jump on me.

"It's about time you showed up," she said. "I know you were awake when I left. Everything okay?"

And then it appeared. That big-eyed look of pity that both Daria and Tiffany had been giving me since my parents left for Texas. They really thought I was living on borrowed time, staying with Daria until her roommate came back, so I could spend one last summer with my best friends before my parents forced me to start my senior year in a brand new school. I'd prove them all wrong.

"Everything's great," I said. "You should be happy that my lack of punctuality has remained intact."

Daria rolled her eyes as only Daria could. She was tall and slender and carried herself like a model. She was wearing a purple and turquoise sundress with a Grecian neckline that made her look like a goddess. The colors were a brilliant contrast for her warm brown skin. Her hair was pulled back into a high ponytail that exploded in a mass of tight black curls. She was, hands-down, the most beautiful person I knew.

"He's here!" Tiffany interrupted the pity-fest, reaching across the desk to squeeze my arm.

"He?" I said, feeling utterly lost for a second. I followed Tiffany's gaze toward the front doors of the library and saw "him" striding in. Marcel, a.k.a. Tiffany's dream come true. She'd been in love with France since we did that group project in the fifth grade, and he was infatuated with her from the moment he'd walked in three months ago to get a library card. Tiffany had heard his French accent, and she was his.

Marcel approached Tiffany with an earnest smile on his face. However, always a gentleman, he broke eye contact with the object of his affection for a moment to acknowledge Daria and me.

"Good morning, ladies," he greeted us.

"Hi, Marcel," we replied, not unlike schoolchildren

greeting their teacher. Tiffany giggled, causing her all-American blonde curls to bounce around her summer-sky eyes. That was all it took to draw Marcel's attention back to her and, for them, suddenly the library didn't exist.

In an attempt to give Tiffany and Marcel a little privacy, I turned toward Daria but froze mid-pivot. A fiery trail sparked along my spine. Even though I didn't see him, I knew Gabriel was looking at me. The thought of him, of those incredible eyes concealed somewhere, watching me, was enough to make me gasp.

"What's up?" Daria asked, her eyes narrowing. "You sure there isn't something wrong?"

Much as I loved Daria, she was a no-nonsense person. She was nineteen, had just finished her freshman year of college and loved her psychology classes. She'd taken to psychoanalyzing Tiffany and me with great relish. Granted, she generally seemed to be on the right track, but this time I wasn't in the mood for the hidden interpretation of why this new guy was affecting me so strongly.

"I might be getting sick," I lied, putting my hand on my stomach for emphasis.

Daria waved me away.

"Don't do it here! Go take a break or something!"

Grateful for a reason to sneak away from the feelings Gabriel could conjure up with just a glance, I made my escape. The staff bathroom was the best haven to compose myself, even if it perpetually smelled of strawberry Jell-O from the ultra-perfumed soap in the dispenser. I splashed cold water on my face until I felt mostly normal again.

When I rejoined the girls at the desk, Tiffany was practically levitating with joy. I said a mental "thank you" to Marcel for doing whatever he'd done to keep the focus off of me.

"Tonight we're watching French films!" Tiffany gushed before I even had a chance to ask. "He's going to come back when my shift is over and take me out for dinner first. Isn't he the best?"

"Look at you!" I grinned. "At this rate, you'll be in France after graduation."

Tiffany crossed her fingers and smiled a dreamy smile.

"Hey," I began, trying to sound casual as I changed the subject. "Did Laura introduce you to the new guy?"

Tiffany puckered her mouth as she tried to think. "New guy… New guy. Oh yeah. I forget his name."

Daria smirked. "I wondered when you would mention him."

"What's that supposed to mean?" I challenged.

"I mean he's fine and you're single."

Leave it to Daria to get to the heart of the matter.

Tiffany waved her hand as if brushing him off. "He's okay, if you're into the dark moody thing. I prefer the clean, confident look of the Frenchman."

Daria and I rolled our eyes at each other.

Tiffany narrowed her eyes but smiled. "Don't tell me you're crushing on Mr. Emo."

"Of course not," I said, sorry I'd brought it up. "I

just think he has really cool eyes."

Tiffany shrugged. "I didn't notice them."

I could feel Tiffany and Daria smiling at each other.

A pang of guilt, better left ignored, caused me to dig myself a little deeper. "Did it occur to you that maybe I can admire Gabriel's eyes without having a crush on him?"

"She remembers his name!" Tiffany stage whispered to Daria. They giggled as I smiled at a woman who was approaching with a stack of books to check out. Happy to tune them out, I focused on doing my job. At least I still had these mundane details of life to worry about.

3

Gabriel

I can't get her out of my head. Every time I blink, her sparkling blue eyes are right there and I'm drawn to her against all reason.

It isn't just the eyes. It's the way she looked at me. There's a tempest going on behind those eyes but she still *sees* me. No one's done that since…

I run my hands through my hair, fighting the impulse to tear it out. Damn, that girl completely got my number the second she looked at me. It was crazy. It was unbelievable. I have to see her again.

I head over to my bookshelf and run a finger over the edges of manila envelopes filed there. Which one should I choose?

Damn, her eyes were amazing. But no, I have to pick an envelope. I shake my head, but it doesn't dislodge the image of her eyes.

I pull out an envelope and remove the few sheets of paper inside; one of my "journal" entries. I skim the lines. Not bad. Maybe she would like it.

No! What am I doing, going insane over this girl? We haven't even talked, I can't just hand her a story the next time I see her. What the hell would I say? "I just met you, but I want you to read this crazy shit I wrote." Yeah, that would be smooth, if I wanted to go to jail, directly to jail. Do not pass Go. No two hundred bucks.

I take a deep breath and return the envelope to the shelf.

Chill out, I tell myself. She's just a girl.

Yeah, right.

There is no way my mind will calm down on its own, so I cross the floor to the medicine cabinet and pull out a bottle of mental health. I swallow one pill and head to my bed. It won't take long to kick in.

I lie flat on my back and stare at the ceiling.

There's so much I want to tell her. Need to tell her. I roll onto my side to face the bookcase again. Which envelope should I start with?

I clench my fists and turn back to the ceiling. No. I'm not starting with any. Why the hell can't I be normal? A normal guy would know how to talk to the most incredible girl he's ever met. He wouldn't freak her out first thing with a stupid story.

The whiteness of the apartment ceiling begins to descend over me like a blanket. That's more like it. My breathing slows and the image of her eyes begins to fade. The cottony stuffing of numbness makes a protective barrier around my brain. With the pill doing its job, I can relax and let go of Christine for a while. I fix my eyes on the ceiling and escape into its consistent white peace as I've done countless times before.

4

Christine

Tiffany and I enjoyed a morning at the park while Daria had brunch with her sister. I didn't have time to waste, so while Tiffany dipped her toes in the pond, I discussed my big plan.

"It's all a matter of a place to stay," I said, squinting at the sunlight on the water's surface.

"Mm-hm," agreed Tiffany, eyes closed, face turned to the sun.

"If I can find a place to live next year, they'll have no choice but to let me. I know Mom is on the fence about the whole thing anyway."

"Maybe Tonya won't come back and you can just keep staying with Daria."

I'd already thought about that possibility, but it probably wasn't likely. Daria's roommate, Tonya, had gone to visit her older sister in Japan for the summer. She'd be back before classes started.

"Tonya's not going to quit school to stay in Japan, although that would be a lot easier for me."

"Maybe you can find someone else with an AWOL roommate," Tiffany suggested.

"Maybe," I conceded. Although, I didn't know how many college students would want to share an apartment with a high school senior. I was lucky that Daria and I were already friends.

"Too bad I can't pretend to be an exchange student like Marcel."

Tiffany perked up at the mention of his name. "Maybe his family would take you in for the year. They have a room they could convert to a bedroom. It's only temporary, after all."

Another unlikely prospect, but I couldn't rule it out.

Tiffany got a wicked gleam in her eye. "You know, if you work on the new guy, maybe you can stay with him for the year."

I punched her playfully in the arm. "Get real, Tiff. I haven't even had a conversation with him."

"You already said he was cute. Go for it."

"I said he had nice eyes."

"Same difference."

Just thinking about his eyes made me shiver. I hugged my knees to my chest to conceal it, but Tiffany had already seen.

"You've got it bad! Just thinking about him makes you all quivery." She grinned and I could see the matchmaking wheels turning in her head.

"Stop. I don't even know him."

"Chemistry doesn't work like that. Besides, you're going to get to know him. Just leave it to me."

I sighed. "I don't have time for this. First, I need a

place to stay. It'll only be worse if I start going out with someone and have to leave him too."

Tiffany slipped her sandals back on and stood up. "You worry too much."

"Where are you going?" I asked, scrambling up after her.

"We've got some things to do before work."

"Like what?"

Tiffany stopped and put her arm around me. "Just trust me."

5

Christine

Protesting had gotten me nowhere. Tiffany strolled into work with me, arm-in-arm, like I was her new prize. Our "some things to do" turned out to be a quick makeover for me. She'd done my hair, makeup and loaned me her favorite red sundress. When I insisted that it was too much, she gave herself a similar treatment. After all, Marcel was bound to stop in sooner or later.

When we turned the corner to the copy room, she turned and made a hasty exit when she saw Gabriel lingering at the mailboxes with a manila envelope in his hand.

"Forgot something!" she called back as she headed toward the lockers.

Alone with Gabriel, I felt ridiculous in my outfit, which Tiffany had chosen precisely to get his attention.

"Hello," he said. Notably, his eyes were on mine. I don't think he even noticed the dress.

His eyes piercing in their intensity, I felt like I might burst into flames beneath their scrutiny. I had to pull myself together. He was a co-worker. If I couldn't bring myself to look at him and speak intelligible words, there would be serious trouble. So I focused on his lips instead of his eyes.

"Hi," I said, with what I hoped was a polite smile. "Did your first day go well?"

It was torturous to string those few words together. Being so close to Gabriel felt like gravitating toward a black hole. I wished fervently to escape before I embarrassed myself.

"It wasn't bad," he said. Still focused on his lips when he spoke those three simple words, a strange twisty feeling nestled in the pit of my stomach. I had to get out of that room before I drowned.

We stood in silence for a moment before I gestured toward my mailbox. "I need my nametag," I said.

Instead of moving away, he pulled out the nametag for me. When I reached for it, our fingers touched. It was like the warmth of his skin traveled straight to my heart and the nametag clattered to the floor.

"Sorry," he said. "I'll get it."

My cheeks flamed with embarrassment. When he stooped down I noticed the envelope in his hand had my name written in spidery letters.

He placed the nametag in my open palm and saw my eyes on the envelope. Now it was his turn to look embarrassed.

"Oh this," he said, holding the envelope toward me slightly. "You don't have to read it." His body leaned a sliver closer to mine so I kept my eyes down and tried to keep my breathing even.

"What is it?" I asked, only looking up briefly to glance at his lips.

"It's just this stupid thing I wrote," he said, running a hand through his hair. "I probably shouldn't have—"

"You write?" I snapped my head up and looked him in the eye. The surprise on his face bolstered my confidence. "I'd love to read it. I like reading." I squeezed my eyes shut. And there it was. I'd finally said something stupid in front of him.

"I guess it's a good thing you work in a library."

I opened my eyes to find Gabriel grinning at me. My insides morphed, briefly, into the consistency of marshmallow.

I laughed. "Yeah, you can tell it's done wonders for my vocabulary."

"Don't worry. You're not the one slipping stories to people you don't know."

"What kind of stuff do you write?"

He looked down and adjusted his stance. "I guess you could say it's mostly dark, flash-fiction-y sort of stuff."

"I like a gothic edge in my reading."

"Really? I had a feeling you'd get it." He looked a little more certain as he offered me the envelope. "Well, it's yours if you really want it."

My fingers itched to tear into it, but I didn't want to make him uncomfortable.

"Thanks," I said. "I can't wait to read it."

We stood, smiling at each other, until Laura walked in. She raised her eyebrows the tiniest bit when she saw me standing there with Gabriel.

"It's a little busy up front," she said.

"Sorry!" I said, embarrassment making me overly enthusiastic. I stuffed the envelope into my box and fumbled to pin on my nametag. Laura started to give Gabriel some tasks for the day and I took my cue to get up to the desk.

Tiffany had sneaked up front by another route and she and Daria were already dealing with a long line of frowny people. I jumped into place and turned my sign to open.

"Are you ready to check out?" I asked a disapproving old woman with deep vertical lines in her face, which made her frown seem impossibly long.

"I am, but are you?" she snapped, dumping her books on the desk with a thump.

Surprised by her surliness, I just stared, at a complete loss for anything helpful to say.

She leaned toward me, her eyebrows becoming severe slashes on her forehead. "Your cheeks are flushed. Your eyes are glassy. Are you on drugs?"

"No!" I exclaimed, the shock making me speak a little louder than I should have. "I was running a little behind and just raced up here as quick as I could, I certainly don't—"

"Is your supervisor here?" she interrupted.

"Actually, sh—" was all I could get out. Gabriel had appeared from outside my range of vision, and approached the woman.

"Is there a problem here?" he asked.

"Yes there is," said the woman, turning to Gabriel. "I think this girl needs a drug test. She's been disruptive and rude." She pulled herself up a little straighter as she spoke, as though making herself better than me with every word.

"If anyone's disruptive and rude, it's you," Gabriel said in an even tone. "We don't tolerate harassment. I'd appreciate it if you left." He looked her dead in the eye and didn't even blink.

The woman, to my amazement, drew an indignant breath, thrust her books at Gabriel and headed toward the door without another word.

I gaped at Gabriel. Like the lady, I didn't know what to say.

He turned to me. "I can't stand rudeness. I'll take care of these books." With no further explanation, he turned and disappeared into the stacks, leaving me speechless.

The next patron in line moved right up, cell phone firmly pressed to his ear. He plopped a stack of books in front of me, which I could only stare at like an idiot. He finally mouthed, "I'm returning," and pointed to the books, like nothing remarkable had just happened.

When we'd finally taken care of everyone in line, Tiffany turned to me.

"I've never seen anything like it!" she whispered.

"Was that the new guy?" asked Daria.

I nodded. "I ran into him earlier. He told me he's a writer." It had nothing to do with the situation, but I didn't know what to say.

Daria frowned. "You don't start a new job and go talking to people like that. If Laura had seen that, he'd be fired on the spot."

"Maybe," Tiffany mused. "But God knows we get enough pissy patrons up here. Wouldn't we all love to do what he did?"

"Yeah," was all I managed to say.

Daria shook her head, still frowning. "That's the sort of thing you only dream about doing. It just isn't professional."

Tiffany shrugged, a smile tugging at her lips. "It's sort of sweet. Maybe not very smart, but he did defend Christine. That's cool."

Daria pressed her lips together and didn't say anything more.

Tiffany gave me a meaningful glance that implied my dress had certainly gotten his attention. I shook my head, hoping she would give it a rest.

We always dealt with grumpy patrons. It was just part of working with the public, but I'd never seen anyone get thrown out before, and especially not by a page. I needed to talk to him again.

"I'm taking a break," I said, not waiting for Tiffany or Daria to acknowledge it. If they noticed I was heading for the stacks instead of the break room, they didn't say anything.

Just when I thought he'd vanished into thin air, I found him, in the romance aisle, shelving the books the woman had left behind.

"Hey," I said when I saw him.

He looked up as I approached.

"Sorry," he said immediately. "I heard that lady hassling you and I couldn't stand it. I didn't mean to get you in trouble or anything."

"Stop," I said. "I'm not in any trouble. I just wanted to say thanks."

His eyes grew wide like he was surprised. I looked down.

"That was really nice of you to help me out. A little risky for a new guy." I glanced up from under my eyelashes and smiled. "But really nice."

His shoulders relaxed and he smiled back. "Yeah, I have an impulsive streak."

"Well, make sure you don't show it to Laura. She's nice, but she takes this place seriously."

"Thanks for the heads up."

"No problem. Well, I'd better get back up there." I turned toward the desk.

"Hey, do you—" Gabriel stopped when I turned back. He shook his head, dismissing whatever he'd been about to ask. "Pretty dress," he mumbled instead.

"Thanks," I said, certain he'd notice the blush erupting on my face that instant.

I had to admit that maybe Tiffany knew what she was doing.

6

Christine

"So what are you going to do about Gabriel?" Tiffany asked.

"What do you mean?" I replied, cradling the phone on my shoulder as I attempted to paint my toenails and talk simultaneously.

Tiffany sighed heavily, like I was trying her patience.

"He's obviously into you," she said. "No way would a guy do what he did if he wasn't interested."

"You know, I almost think he wanted to ask me out but changed his mind."

Tiffany squealed. "I knew it! This is going to be simple."

"Easy for you to say. You're not the one who's supposed to move across the country in a few weeks."

"Whatever," she said. "You're the one with the grand plan."

I ignored the note of sarcasm in her voice. "Speaking of which, I should go work on that right now. My mom was texting me pictures of carpet choices for my bedroom. I don't even want to go there."

Tiffany groaned in sympathy. "If I could convince my parents to buy me a bunk bed, I'd move you in right now."

"I know," I said. I'd known Tiffany and her family forever, but they had a three-bedroom home and five people. Tiffany's room was like a closet and her brothers shared a room not much bigger. It just wouldn't work out. Not for a whole year.

"You'll find something," Tiffany said. "I know you will."

Her vote of confidence bolstered my own. We hung up and I finished my nails.

Daria had gone out with her boyfriend, Javier, leaving me with the apartment to myself.

I'd read Gabriel's story over a dozen times, but instead of apartment hunting, I picked up the paper again.

103 by Gabriel Gray

"The sun doesn't shine in hell," I thought. "So, I must be someplace better than that." The sun beat down from the sky as though its sole purpose was to roast me. I squinted into the distance searching for shelter but only saw a red figure coming toward me. As it drew closer, I could see it was a robed man.

"Who are you? Why are you here?" he asked when he reached me.

I raised my hands in a gesture of helplessness. "I don't know. I didn't mean to come here."

"Who are you?" shouted the man, angry this time.

"I'm Nobody," I replied. "I didn't come here by my own will."

"Nobody!" The man in robes shook his head. "I've heard of you. You're dangerous."

"No," I said. "I'm not dangerous, just unfortunate. Believe me, I won't hurt you."

"Why would I trust you?" the man asked. "Your story precedes you. No place you visit is safe. Where you arrive, trouble follows."

"It's not my doing," I said. "I swear it. I don't know why this curse is upon me."

"Then you must take your curse and go away from everyone. You are not welcome here."

"Please, can you help me?" I fell to my knees in the dust of the road. "I don't want to travel this path anymore. I only want to go home."

The man considered my plea for a moment. Then shook his head. "There is no home for you. You dwell in the eye of the storm. Trouble dances all around you. No one will take you because they'd have to accept the storm as well. I wish you a short life so your suffering will end. Until then, leave here and keep to yourself."

The man turned his back and retraced the way he'd come.

I remained kneeling in the dust, but now I understood. I would always be alone.

I carefully set it on the nightstand, too drained for my great plan, and climbed into bed. Why did it seem like these words spoke directly to what had happened at the library?

It was queasy scary. Not the horror movie kind of fear, rather an enticing dread. It hinted at darkness below the surface. It was disturbing and damaged but not entirely beyond redemption.

The last line of Gabriel's story echoed in my brain. My mind conjured a detailed memory of his full lips and put those words in his mouth, "I would always be alone." Just as I began to drift off to sleep, the words changed to a plea.

"Please don't leave me alone."

7

Christine

I walked down a moonlit street. It smelled like smoldering autumn leaves but there was no chill in the air. Wind slowly blew through the trees and made their leaves whisper. Everything else was quiet.

The wind curled around me, but this time it brought a few drops of rain with it. Glancing at the sky, I noticed clouds gathering over the moon. It dawned on me that I should get back home and go to bed. I looked around and, for the first time, realized I wasn't in my neighborhood. This neighborhood resembled a set from a musical rather than a real street. The houses were big and imposing, like something from *My Fair Lady*. At any moment, I expected to see Rex Harrison and Audrey Hepburn strolling toward me. The thought of wandering through an old movie scene, alone, at night caused cold goose bumps to rise on my arms. *Keep it together, Christine.* I tried to stay reasonable.

Was it safer to go back the way I'd come or keep going into unknown territory? I didn't remember going for a walk anyway. Basically, turning back was no different than continuing on. I took another quick scan of the street to see if anyone else was out. Nothing stirred. Even the wind had deserted me.

I tried to grab hold of my courage. There had to be a logical explanation for this and it wasn't like I could have wandered too far from home. I decided my best bet was to turn around and go the way I'd apparently come. Maybe something would look familiar eventually and I'd be snuggled in my bed soon.

I turned and the wind rushed past my ears. "Christine," it sighed, producing the effect of ice water dripping down my spine. The voice was soft, but I had not imagined it.

"Who said that?" I asked. I half expected a deceased relative to materialize before my eyes and give me a message from beyond. Instead, my words fell into the emptiness of night and disappeared. The wind picked up again, but this time it was silent. I knew I'd heard a voice so I started walking as fast as I could while trying to look nonchalant. Each house I walked past looked identical to the last: two-story Victorian homes, empty driveways leading to closed garages, same eight wooden steps before the front door, big picture window to the right of the door, all windows dark.

Just as I began to think a scream would explode from my mouth, I noticed something different. Up ahead a few houses, one picture window had a light shining inside. I didn't know if it was a good or bad sign. I crossed to the opposite side of the road from the house so I wouldn't be too close when I walked past. Perhaps I could sneak a glance inside and remain undetected. As I reached the window, I tried to keep my head down and only turn my eyes. I didn't want to obviously stare into someone's home in the middle of the night. A thin woman in a threadbare pink bathrobe and unkempt blonde hair walked back and forth with a crying baby. Her head bowed over the baby and her lips moved slowly, as if she were singing a lullaby.

The woman must have sensed she was being watched because she suddenly looked up, right at me. Fear turned my body to stone. The woman and I stared at each other for a moment before she smiled, weary, but friendly. Before I could react, she gently extracted the baby from its cozy spot nestled under her chin and held it up to me. It had stopped crying and looked straight at me with stunning brown eyes. Both baby and mother seemed to hold an unasked question in their eyes. As I tried to decipher what they could want, the wind snaked through my hair.

"Christine!" it sang suddenly, like a discordant Hallelujah chorus. I jolted upright in bed, soaked with sweat. I gulped air like I'd been drowning and my senses began to come back to me. The dull red numbers of my alarm clock showed 2:34 am. It had been a dream. The street, the wind, the baby, none of it was real. I shivered and pulled the sheet up over my head. I couldn't crack now. Not when I needed to fix my life in one summer. Not when I'd just met someone as intriguing as Gabriel.

8

Gabriel

I hear voices on the beach, too close for comfort. Boots stomp through wet sand. I whip my head around, expecting to discover them right behind me but I don't see anyone yet. Sometimes, it takes a while for visuals to kick in. One thing is clear; they're after me.

"Gabriel," a woman calls my name (how the hell does she know my name?) and I book it into the fringe of trees that lines the beach as far as I can see. A branch scratches the hell out of my cheek, but I don't have time to care until I'm safe in the dense foliage of a well-placed bush.

Peering out from my shelter, I catch sight of them, right where I'd been standing. Damn, they're close, two of them, a guy and a girl. They walk together, heads swiveling in every direction as they look for me. I try not to look directly at them. It'd be just my luck they'd feel me watching them and come straight for me.

"Gabriel, are you here?" calls the girl.

I don't answer. She looks short enough that I could take her if I have to, but she also has a spiky-hair Anime chick vibe going on that I don't want to mess with.

"We want to help you," yells the guy.

Yeah, right. I don't need any help from him. He's built like a quarterback. He could easily crush me beneath one of his damn boots. Anime chick would probably go flying through the air to land a drop kick to my jaw. Then they'd both wipe their boots on my face and go off to "help" some other innocent schmuck. No thanks.

They continue along the beach until the guy shrugs.

"We'll never find him here. Let's head back and check the frequency."

The girl grunts her frustration. "I was sure he was here."

And boom, they vanish.

I'm left alone, hiding in the bush, wishing I could vanish at will.

A pair of seagulls screech overhead and land to fight over some nasty morsel washed up at the water's edge. I watch their antics until the whole beach scene begins to fade and I feel my body coming back to me. In all the years I've been doing this, I never feel the difference until the real, physical awareness comes back. It starts with the sensation of my clothes against my skin, usually followed by the weight of my organs filling my body. Every time is like the first, even though I always swear I'll never forget again. This is what being alive feels like. I open my eyes, to make sure I'm really back in my own bed. I drift back to sleep, knowing it's only a matter of time before they reach me.

9

Christine

The next time I walked into work, a new story was waiting in my mailbox. I wanted to tear into the envelope immediately but didn't want to get caught. Getting stories from Gabriel was one thing, advertising it to the world was another.

When I got to the desk, the library appeared empty. Daria was surfing the web on her workstation. "Gonna be a slow one," she said without looking up.

Tiffany grinned at me from her computer. "Marcel wants to hang out after work."

Daria smirked. "Tell us something we don't know."

"Who would have thought you could pick up a hot French guy while working at the library?" I mused.

"I know!" agreed Tiffany. "I could be the poster girl for library romance."

"Hey," Daria said, turning to me. "Tiffany's ditching for Marcel, but do you still want to come with me to Javier's poetry reading?"

I'd forgotten about the reading. Daria and Javier were the cutest couple, the kind you can imagine still holding hands when they're old. Tiffany and I had gone to a couple of Javier's readings before. Even though I wasn't the type to curl up with a book of poetry for fun, I could tell Javier had talent.

Before I could figure out if I wanted to go or not, a light sparkled in Tiffany's eyes and a mischievous smile spread over her face.

"I've got it!"

Daria and I turned, awaiting Tiffany's words of wisdom.

"You should bring Gabriel to the reading. It's perfect!"

"No way!" said Daria. "She doesn't need to be encouraging that boy. He's got issues."

"Oh, please. He told an old bag to get off her case. That's chivalrous." Tiffany was on a roll now, but Daria was never one to sit by when she had a point to make.

"It was stupid," Daria said. "It might be chivalrous if he'd known her for a long time, but the first week of work? Not normal."

Tiffany put her hands on her hips, clearly not willing to budge.

"Just bring him to the reading, get to know him a little better and find out who's right."

"I don't want to mess around with that boy," Daria said.

"Of course you don't," Tiffany replied. "But maybe Christine does."

Daria stiffened and then she and Tiffany both fixed me in their expectant gazes.

"I wouldn't mind a chance to talk to him," I said,

feeling a little sheepish. Daria was a great friend, but she could be intimidating sometimes. "But I don't think the poetry reading is the way to go. Not really a place to chat, you know?"

"Hmm," said Tiffany with a slight frown. "Good point." It didn't take her long to brighten again. "Hey, we could all go out for ice cream after work. Then Daria can go to the reading, I can go out with Marcel and you can do whatever." I swear she wanted to wink.

"Listen," Daria said, ignoring Tiffany. "Just because you're mad at your parents for moving away, it doesn't mean you have to start dating a bad boy."

Classic Daria psychoanalysis.

"I'm not looking for a bad boy," I tried to reassure her. "I think Tiffany's right. If we all go out together, it's a nice, safe way to get to know him. If he seems like trouble after that, I'll forget it."

Tiffany beamed.

The hard set of Daria's jaw made it clear she wasn't enthused at all. Lucky for her, I wasn't finished.

"But," I added. "I don't think tonight's the night. Time's ticking for me to find a place to stay and I'd rather get some work done on that before I ask out any new guys or go to the poetry reading."

"Fair enough," Daria was quick to reply.

Tiffany sighed. "Is it really that hard to find an apartment?"

I loved her, but sometimes I really wanted to slap her.

"Finding an apartment is easy. Finding an

apartment I can afford on what I make here is a different story," I explained.

"And that's your excuse to not ask out the guy who's so obviously into you right now?" It was clear where Tiffany's priorities were.

"Since the guy situation won't be a factor if I'm living on the other side of the country, I think I'll take things one step at a time."

Daria couldn't help but smile.

"You're so logical sometimes!" Tiffany exclaimed. "It breaks my romantic heart."

"One step at a time," I repeated, relieved I'd managed to deflect the whole situation for another day.

✳✳✳✳

At last, I was alone in my car with Gabriel's envelope. Its presence filled the passenger seat as much as any human would.

Free for the evening, I didn't really want to spend it alone at Daria's. I sped down the road to my favorite park. The summer sun was rapidly sinking beyond the horizon, throwing the world into shadow. A gentle breeze tickled the branches of my favorite willow tree and beckoned me to enjoy my reading beneath them.

The envelope clutched in one hand, I parted the branches with the other and made my way to the little bench inside. I'd spent many an afternoon beneath those branches dreaming, wishing and pondering.

I sat down, unable to restrain myself from finally tearing into the envelope. Tilting the pages to catch the fast failing light and holding them close to my face, I read:

119 by Gabriel Gray

Walking through the empty house, I tried to remember what it felt like to be a baby there. The bare gray walls and scratched hardwood floors did little to conjure warm happy memories. In fact, I didn't know if there were any happy moments to dredge up, anyway. All I knew, somehow, was that I'd lived here for a brief time. Was it with a loving family who was missing me now? Perhaps my parents had left me immediately and I'd never known them at all. Not even a stolen glance at my mother's face after I was born. It was impossible to tell.

I paused, running my hand along a doorframe of a small bedroom. Had this been my very first room? Did it matter?

I continued walking down the dusty hallway when a searing image struck me with the force of a fist: a flash of light and the sound of a gunshot. I shook my head and staggered back a step. Was I losing my mind? No one else was in the house.

I took a few more steps and peered into what looked like the master bedroom. Another flash: a cheerful bedroom decorated in creams and yellows. The type of place I was hoping for. I took a step into the room and the images and sounds assaulted me, like machine gun fire: "Hide!" A tall, squarish man rose from the bed, where he'd been sitting, lacing his shoes.

A woman pushed herself up from under the blanket. "What do you mean?" she asked, panic laced in her voice.

"They're coming."

"What?" she whispered as her face turned the color of death.

"Get the baby and hide!" The urgency in his voice floated through the room and blew over me like an icy wind. I shuddered and tried to leave, but I couldn't move from the spot.

The woman sprang from the bed, wearing nothing more than a thin nightgown and ran straight through me as if either she or I were a ghost. I felt a twinge of cold as she disappeared into me, then nothing but my own pulsating terror.

With the woman gone, the man took a pistol from the top shelf of the closet and also passed through me. This was worse than the woman. The man was my height. His eyes seemed to stare into mine with a ferocity that made me nauseous. I couldn't look away. My guts wrenched with the transient impact, like walking through a humming electric shock. My stomach heaved in vain, but I had no time to worry about sickness.

Next, indistinct shouting, a flash and a painfully loud sound like an explosion. I felt like a piece of my heart had shattered with the impact of the bullet. The man crumpled to the hardwood floor, his head landing with a crack. Blood began to pool around my feet. Horror shuddered my stomach until I did vomit. It broke the spell.

The bright room faded to nothingness, but my ears

flooded with competing sounds: screaming, children laughing, a family singing "Happy Birthday," a couple fighting, over and over the sound of the gun. I ran, screaming, from the house as fast as I could.

Putting more distance between the house and myself, the sounds grew fainter until they died away altogether. I kept running until a stitch in my side threatened to crush me to the pavement. I wrapped my arms around my stomach, wishing I could keep myself together with my own two hands. My ears hummed with the same fullness I'd experienced after loud concerts. My eyes burned with tears I couldn't shed.

Is this all there is for me? Safe havens that turn into vipers' nests?

When will it ever stop?

The words, beautiful and sickening, wrung my heart into an aching, twisted knot.

I scanned the story over and over, trying to tease out the truth of its author from the fiction of the words. Once I felt like the words had been burned into my brain, I closed my eyes and tried to imagine what it would be like to have a person go through me. Lost in the creepy fantasy, it took me awhile to register the footsteps shushing through the grass behind me.

10

Christine

I jumped up, knocking the story and envelope to the ground. My legs felt like over-stretched elastic when I registered who was standing in front of me.

"Gabriel? What are you doing here?"

The last orange rays of light played through the branches and illuminated patches of his face and body, leaving him more mysterious than ever.

"Christine," he said in a low voice that made my heart pound. "I didn't realize anyone was here. I'll go."

"No!" I exclaimed, reaching toward him, even though the bench was between us.

He stared at me, looking uncertain.

"I just read your last story," I said and bent down to retrieve it from the grass.

He stepped around the bench, cautiously, and crouched down to help me. Our hands brushed together and I dropped the papers again.

"I scare you," he said.

"No," I said, gathering up the pages properly. "Your story, it just—"

"Freaked you out," he finished.

I shook my head. "No, that's not it. I think you're an amazing writer. The ideas, the images, they're just haunting. I don't know what to say."

He stood up. "You could always say, 'Get lost, freak.'"

I stared up at him, shocked.

"I'd never say that."

He ran his hands through his dark hair and sighed.

"I'm doing an excellent job of being an asshole. I'm sorry."

He offered a hand to help me up and I took it.

Once on my feet, we stood awkwardly for a few moments until he broke the silence.

"So," he began, "You really liked those crazy stories?"

"Yes," I agreed, cautious to keep things from spiraling downward again. "The subjects are pretty dark, but you make them beautiful."

"Thank you," he said, looking down. "Not everyone's into dark."

"I'm not everyone," I quipped.

"Yeah. I knew that the first time I saw you."

There was no doubt I was blushing so I looked down and started tracing a circle in the grass with my toe.

"Sorry," he said, running his hand through his hair again. "I just say things sometimes—"

"No," I stopped him. "That's a really great thing to say, I just…" Words failed me.

Gabriel leaned forward, like he wanted to touch

me, but changed his mind and turned away.

"Is something wrong?" I asked.

"Christine," he started, not really looking at me, "you seem like a really great girl, but I want to tell you upfront, I'm not your average guy."

Tension seized my body as I tried to proceed with caution. "I noticed."

"Yeah, I know you noticed. Everyone notices, but you're different. You're willing to give me a chance. Most people aren't." He paused and I thought of Daria's strong dismissal of him.

"I want you to know right now," he continued. "I get into a lot of trouble because people don't understand me. I don't want to get you in any trouble."

Finally, he turned to look at me and I met his gaze. The uncertainty in his eyes captivated me. His mention of "trouble" echoed in my brain. So there was at least a grain of truth in those bizarre stories. But what parts?

"You're right to put your guard up," he continued.

"I haven't even said anything," I replied.

"You don't have to. I can tell. You don't know me and you have no reason to trust me, but I really want to know you." He looked down to his own fidgeting hands. "I just have this feeling…" The words he wasn't saying hung thick in the hot air.

My heart pounded so fiercely, my entire body pulsed with the beat.

"I know what you mean," I said in a very quiet voice. His eyes shot to mine, looking a little incredulous.

"Let me get this straight," Gabriel said. "You didn't

think I was nuts when I told that old lady to get off your case?"

I shrugged. "It was risky for a new guy, but I appreciated it."

"Okay," he continued. "And it didn't bother you that I gave you some weird stories out of the blue?"

"No. I mean, I was surprised, but it didn't bother me." I tucked a lock of hair behind my ear. "It's kinda flattering that you would trust me to read your work."

A small smile lightened his face and stabbed my heart. Despite Daria's warning, despite the red flags waving fiercely all around him, there was something in him that called to me.

"You have incredible eyes," I blurted out before I could censor myself. Horrified, I clamped my hand over my mouth to keep it from saying any more inappropriate things.

Gabriel's smile widened into a real smile, the first full smile I'd seen from him.

My heart fluttered away on hummingbird wings.

He reached out and gently tugged against my wrist, pulling my hand from my betraying lips. The place where his flesh intersected mine undulated with a living energy.

I gasped and dropped my hand from my face.

"You feel the same way, don't you?" he whispered.

Unsure of what to say, I nodded my affirmation.

His eyes probed mine, charged with intensity, but I didn't look away. Their pull was magnetic; I swayed and leaned toward him. He did the same. I examined the autumn amber flecks in the deep brown of his irises, my heartbeat a throbbing freight train in my chest.

His face eclipsed the park and all I could see was him, inches away. My throat went dry and raging blood roared through my ears. I swallowed, thickly, and our slow gravitational pull to each other stopped.

We breathed, inhabiting the same space for a moment before he tenderly reached up and brushed my cheek with a fingertip. I could feel the sparks sizzling from the point of contact even if I couldn't see them.

He held up his finger to show my eyelash resting delicately on the tip.

His lips formed an "O" and, turning his head to the side, blew the eyelash from its perch.

"I think my wish is already coming true," he murmured.

My throat was too dry to speak.

"Come here," he beckoned. "Will you walk with me?"

In no hurry to leave him, I agreed.

It was quickly getting too dark to see, but I knew the park well. We were heading toward the trail into the forest. I leaned closer to Gabriel so that our shoulders bumped into each other every few steps. Gently, he pressed his palm against my back. "Careful," he whispered. "The path is uneven here."

It didn't take long to fall into a comfortable rhythm with Gabriel's footsteps. The trees were like deep black sentinels standing against a star-speckled sky. I paid attention to the trail beneath my feet. Each step had to be carefully planted so as to not be caught off guard by the terrain of wood chips and tree roots. Except for the twinkling stars above the branches, the darkness had become so complete that it was easy to imagine our bodies didn't exist. That only our spirits were floating among and within everything.

Gabriel tenderly took my hand, and the faint silhouette of our joined hands mingled with the dark of the trees, with the sky overhead, the earth below. The ancient pulse of the universe hummed around and through us.

It wasn't until he pulled me back that I realized we'd come to the edge of the river. A river I'd walked beside countless times before, but never like this.

Gabriel took his hand from mine and I heard him shuffling around in the wood chips.

"What are you doing?" I asked.

"Going wading," he replied. "Want to come?"

I slipped my shoes off and, rejoining hands, we stumbled into the unknown together. We made it out, almost to the middle, the water just to our knees.

"Look up," Gabriel urged.

Insulated by the forest, there were no lights, other than those in the heavens. The stars filled the sky with pinpricks of light. The water reflected everything in the sky, creating the illusion of being surrounded by stars.

I turned to Gabriel and was exhilarated when I felt his perfect lips press against mine. I'd felt tingling when he'd looked at me, but this was so much more than that.

It was like we'd been assumed into space, and stars of electricity swirled all around us, sometimes getting too close and sparking on our skin.

When we finally pulled away, both of us were breathless.

I leaned my head on Gabriel's shoulder to gaze at the stars until standing in the cold water made me start to shiver.

"Come on," Gabriel said. "We should get you out of here."

I didn't protest.

Back on the shore, he stripped off his t-shirt and offered it to me as a towel for my legs and feet.

"I don't want to get your shirt all wet!" I said, but he wouldn't listen.

"It's fine, I promise."

I patted my feet dry, just enough to get them into my shoes for the walk back.

We walked silently, hand in hand, until we reached the dimly lit parking lot. Our cars were the only two left.

I tried not to look at his bare chest.

"This was the best night of my life," Gabriel said.

"Me too," I agreed.

Now that we could see each other in the lights, we both seemed to feel shy and uncertain.

"Can I call you sometime?" he asked, running a hand through his hair.

"Of course!" I said, fumbling for my phone so we could exchange numbers. Once that was done, and not quite knowing what else to do, I pulled my keys from my pocket.

"I guess I should go."

Gabriel nodded. "Yeah, me too." There was an awkward moment when he looked like he wanted to kiss me again, but my eyes flicked to his bare chest and he looked self-conscious, even though he certainly had nothing to be embarrassed about.

"Goodnight for now," I said. "Sweet dreams."

"Sweet dreams," he echoed, meaning it more than I could ever have imagined.

11

Gabriel

I pull out of the parking spot at the park and I am on fire. No, not fire. I'm buzzing with the energy of Christine.

Oh God! She's like no one else in the world and she feels it too! This is unprecedented. How could I accidentally land this library job, meet this amazing girl and have this incredible moment in the park with her? My luck has completely changed. I don't know how, but something major has shifted here. Can I dare to believe I get to have someone good in my life again?

Shit! I slam down on my brakes when I realize, almost too late, that I'm coming up on a red light. The tires squeal against the pavement and I brace myself for the telltale thud.

I am spared, by about an inch, from rear-ending the guy ahead of me. From the light of the signal, I see him flip me off. I throw my hands up and mouth "sorry," but I don't think he even notices.

A lead weight pushes down in my stomach. The high from kissing Christine has already worn off and I know that I'm going to pay. Somehow, I'm going to pay dearly for this moment of respite. It's the only thing I can count on.

12

Christine

A light breeze blew up from behind me on the deserted street. Wearing jeans and a t-shirt, the breeze gave me a sudden chill. I folded my arms over my chest and looked around. There were silent houses on either side of the street. The dark windows gaped at me in a way that made me self-conscious.

The breeze blew again and a little spiral of dead leaves scratched around my feet. I looked behind me and the scene was exactly the same as in front of me. It seemed like this silent street stretched on into infinity.

There was a vague sense of familiarity, but I couldn't quite fit the pieces together. More curious than frightened, I slowly walked on, trying to figure out how I knew it.

At last, the scratching of the leaves was interrupted by the muffled sound of voices. I stopped to pinpoint their location. It seemed to be ahead, so I jogged up a little way and the sound became clearer. A woman was shouting, but I couldn't tell which house it was coming from. I scanned each side of the street but none of the houses looked any different. All had closed doors and black windows. No lights. No movement. Since I couldn't see anything, I strained to understand what she was yelling. I continued walking, trying to get a better vantage point.

After what felt like a good fifteen minutes of waiting, a door opened a few houses up on the right and someone was shoved out onto the wooden planks of the porch. I could hear the woman clearly now. "I don't know what the hell you think you're doing, but you better stay away from this house! I'm calling the police, you son of a bitch!"

The door slammed but the person huddled on the porch didn't move. Before I could even think, my legs were running to the porch. It was a stupid compulsion, but I had to see if the person was all right. The way he or she just lay there didn't sit well with me.

As I ran up the steps, the young man, as I now saw he was, kept his head down and back to me. I came to a full stop, almost toppling over.

"Gabriel!"

His head snapped up when I called his name. An ugly bruise darkened his cheek.

"What are you doing? Let's get out of here," I said as I grabbed his arms to help him up.

"Christine? What are you doing here?" Gabriel's voice shook. He didn't make any attempt to stand up, just looked at me like I was a ghost.

"I'm trying to get you out of here before that lady comes back."

Gabriel glanced at the front door and seemed to

become himself. He jumped up, grabbed my hand, and we ran as fast as we could. Sprinting down the street of sameness until we finally found something different: the edge of a forest. We veered into it and finally stopped to hide under some bushes. We sat, out of breath, for a while before either of us said anything. Gabriel still held my hand.

"Where are we?" I whispered when I couldn't stand it any longer.

Gabriel took a deep breath and pushed his hair back. He took my other hand, holding both of them to his chest.

"Christine, don't think I'm crazy for asking this, but are you…really here?"

"Of course I am." My voice betrayed a hint of annoyance. After seeing him get kicked out of an angry woman's house, the reality of my presence was the least of my concerns.

He didn't say anything for a moment, but he didn't break eye contact. His eyes were filled with emotions I couldn't interpret. He took another deep breath and spoke solemnly.

"Did you ever wonder where I got the idea for those stories I gave you?"

I didn't see how story inspiration had anything to do with crouching in the unfamiliar woods, but I humored him.

"Yes," I answered.

His eyes stayed on me, searching for something. The intensity would have made me blush if I wasn't feeling so nervous. He'd warned me about trouble, but I never would have imagined this. My eyes strayed to the bruise on his face. It was beginning to swell. We'd have to get some ice on it soon.

Finally, he spoke but his tone was uncertain.

"Well, I write about things that have happened to me." He paused, looking like he was trying to figure out how to go on while monitoring my reaction.

My mind raced as I tried to recall the details of the stories. Hadn't he said he'd walked through a person? What about the robed man who hoped he'd die? That had to be symbolic for something. Those things couldn't really happen.

Clouds of doubt gathered in Gabriel's eyes and his face went tight with worry. Crouched in the woods, the trouble he'd alluded to seemed a lot more menacing than in the dreamy sunset of a willow tree. Clearly, we were both in trouble now, but panic wasn't an option.

"It's okay," I encouraged him. "You can tell me anything."

Gabriel's brow was deeply furrowed, his eyebrows anxious dashes on his face. Whatever it was, he was afraid to tell me.

"Let me explain it this way," he started. "Do you know how you got here?"

I tried to think backward: finding Gabriel on the porch, the woman yelling, the silence, that strange street. I couldn't get beyond that point. When I didn't answer, he continued.

"What's your last memory before you found

yourself here?"

It took some reaching, but I finally came up with a senseless answer. "Well, this is crazy, but my last memory is getting back to my apartment after being in the park with you." I wrinkled up my face. "That can't be right, though." I looked around the forest, at the dusky light of day filtering through the dense leaves. It was already dark when I got back to my apartment. How could it be early twilight here? Fear's shadowy fingers began to slither up from my toes.

"What is going on?" I demanded with a harshness born of fear.

Gabriel lowered his face a little closer to mine and whispered. "Christine, you're going to think I'm psycho, but I swear I'm telling the truth. This isn't easy to say, but…" His mouth was open but he didn't go on.

"Gabriel, just tell me." I tried to brace myself for whatever he might say.

"This is a dream," he said so quietly I almost didn't hear him. His eyes bored into mine, desperate to find my reaction. A dream? Had he seriously said we were in a dream? Forcing myself to remain calm, I turned my eyes back to the forest around us.

Nothing indicated a dream. The setting sun cast shadows through the trees and highlighted the delicate veins in the leaves and ridges of the bark. I could smell the crisp dusk air and Gabriel's soapy clean scent. I let go of his hands and encircled one of his wrists. I could feel the rhythmic pulsing of the blood through his veins. I slowly turned my eyes back to his.

"It sounds insane, I know, but I also know we're both back in our homes, sleeping."

I couldn't comprehend what he was saying. I'd been aware of dreaming before but it didn't feel the same as sitting in those woods.

Gabriel went on. "We're dreaming, but this is completely real. I live in two realities. I've been doing it since I was eight, but I've always been alone. I don't understand how you're here."

I knew I should say something, but I couldn't find any words. It was terrifying that I had no memory of coming to this place and that I'd found Gabriel getting thrown out of some woman's house, but a dream? I let go of Gabriel's wrist and rubbed my forehead. Was I hallucinating or something?

Gabriel nervously ran a hand through his hair and started talking fast. "I know your mind is going a mile a minute. Mine did when I first realized what was going on. All I know is that when I fall asleep, I'm going to end up somewhere, alone, where I'm not wanted. This time I was behind the sofa in that woman's house. She discovered me and hit me in the face with a broom." He indicated the hideous bruise on his cheek. "I've been to all sorts of places, but most aren't fun. Something always feels wrong. I don't always interact with someone, and I don't always get hurt, but I always feel so completely alone. That's the worst part, and it spills over into my "normal" life. I mean, who can relate to the freak that lives another life when he's dreaming? I can't even relate to myself."

He started fidgeting with his hands. "I'm rambling, Christine. Please, please, tell me what you're thinking." His eyes were back on mine, pleading. We stared at each other in silence. I didn't know what to think, let alone what to say. I could only ground myself in one thing: his eyes begging me to not reject him. I didn't know the right thing to say, but I didn't want to say the wrong thing either. Every word seemed so critical all of a sudden.

Finally, my mind stumbled upon a question that I thought was adequate. "How do we get out of here?" I sounded scared, even to my own ears.

None of the anxiety left his eyes. "I don't know. Sometimes I get out and have regular dreams and wake up like a normal person. Other times I stay here all night and don't wake up until my alarm goes off. Sometimes, not even then. I'm just sort of here until this place is done with me."

"Could we not talk about sleep right now?" was all I could formulate.

Gabriel looked like I'd just kicked him in the throat. I'd said the wrong thing. I didn't have time to backpedal. Police sirens started to howl. I jumped to Gabriel's side and clutched his arm. There was nothing else I could hold on to.

"She called the police. We need to stay hidden," Gabriel whispered, crouching lower to the ground. I followed his lead. Too frightened to speak, I hugged his arm as tightly as I could. He reached over and laced his fingers through mine and then we both kept motionless, eyes riveted on the street.

A cop car stopped just in front of the woods. I didn't dare to breathe in case it would give us away.

The window of the squad car rolled down and the officer lowered his mirrored glasses. For a moment, my heart froze. I swore he stared directly into my eyes. I couldn't move or breathe as I watched his dull blue eyes slowly sweep the forest. He gave the impression of being able to see through every leaf, under every bush. My thumping heart clogged my throat, threatening to choke me.

After a lifetime of terrified waiting, the window rolled back up and the police car slowly pulled away.

I turned to Gabriel and fell backward when I discovered he wasn't there. There was no sign that he'd been crouched in the bushes with me at all. It was lucky the cop was gone because my gasp would have given me away.

I sprang to my feet, not sure what to do. I started running deeper into the woods. Branches scratched my face and pulled my hair. Roots tried to trip me with almost every step. I didn't know what I was running to, but I knew it was better than sitting still, doing nothing but waiting for my fate to be sealed. The longer I ran, the faster I seemed to go until everything was a brownish-green blur in my periphery. I felt like I was no longer in a forest, but in a tunnel that was slowly closing in around me. Just when I got to the point where the walls were about to crush me, I screamed, and it was over.

13

Gabriel

I have never hated myself so much.

Of all the times to be miraculously spared from danger, why the hell did it have to be tonight…when she needs me?

What if she screamed? What if the cop found her and he's…no. I can't even think it.

I am such a screw up!

Why did I give Christine those damn stories? Why did I think I had any right to talk to her? I should have left her the hell alone. She barely looked at me when we met. Why didn't I take the hint and walk away? No, her eyes were so amazing, she seemed so wonderful I just had to insert myself into her nice little life and totally mess it up.

She shouldn't be in the dreamworld. That's my personal hell, not hers. I've got to get her out of there. I have to make this right.

My sheet tangles around me, like a tether, as I try to get out of bed. I have to call her, but even my damn bed is conspiring against me.

In my haste, I rip the sheet and stumble onto the floor.

One hand fumbles for my cell on the bookshelf while I push myself up with the other hand. It doesn't take long to find her number, hers is the first one I put in my phone.

Ring.

Pick up.

Ring.

Christine, pick up.

Ring.

This has to work.

Ring.

Please…

14

Christine

My body felt like a jigsaw puzzle being put togeth-er. I could feel the weight of my organs. Feel the structured scaffolding of my bones and muscles, my skin finally tightening around the whole package.

Next came audio. As if floating to me from a long way off, a sound started out distant and undecipher-able, until finally I recognized my cell ringing. I opened my eyes and saw the dark outline of my bedroom. I felt the mattress underneath me. I turned to my nightstand where I saw the red numbers of the alarm clock: 2:23 am.

A knock on my bedroom door pulled me all the way back to the real world.

"Christine," Daria rasped at the door. "You all right in there?"

"Yeah," I called back. "Just a nightmare. Sorry I woke you."

My cell went to voicemail and I would have for-gotten it if it didn't start ringing again immediately. Although the ring tone was the same as always, it felt panicked.

"Is your phone ringing?"

I snatched it off my nightstand and turned it off. "Sorry!"

"Can I come in?" Daria asked.

"Of course."

Daria stepped into my dark room. "Is something going on?"

"No," I said. "Just a bad dream. I can't believe I woke you up."

"Yeah," she said, coming in and sitting gently at the edge of my bed. "You were screaming. Scared the hell out of me."

"Really?" I exclaimed, genuinely embarrassed. "That's never happened to me before."

Daria sighed. "Little more stressed out than you let on?"

I thought about my parents. About how I was supposed to say goodbye to Tiffany and Daria and disappear to Texas, without any friends at all.

I didn't like to admit that the whole situation scared me to death.

Grateful for the cover of darkness, I let a couple tears slide down my cheeks.

"I guess so." My voice wobbled.

"It's gonna be all right, Christine," Daria said, patting my leg. "Even if you move, it's only for a year. Once you're eighteen, you can do whatever you want. You can come back to Michigan and go to Eastern for college, just like you planned. Tiffany and I will still be here. It's only a year."

Her words made sense, but even a year, senior year, was longer than I wanted to be away.

"I kinda hate my parents for this," I said.

Daria laughed, low and quiet. "Girl, you're seventeen years old. You're supposed to hate your parents."

I leaned over to poke her in the arm. "Don't call me 'girl.'" Even though I felt like one at that moment.

Daria patted my leg before heading back to the door.

"You're smart. You're gonna make it work."

"I hope you're right," I sighed.

"Of course I'm right," she laughed softly. "Now, go back to sleep."

It sounded simple enough, but sleep wouldn't return. Every time I'd start to doze off, I'd be jolted awake by some horrific image. As night continued, the images became more twisted until I finally found myself strolling along the moors of England at dusk. Wearing a long, coarse dress, shawl and bonnet, I fancied I had become Jane Eyre. Straining to see past an area of trees and large rocks, I imagined my love, waiting there to greet me. Filled with excitement, I picked my way through the tall whispering grass. Finally, I would be able to embrace my beloved Rochester without fear of being caught by the madwoman. It was exhausting trying to keep ahead of her and her violent obsessions. Tonight, a secret tryst would be our reward for steadfast love.

As I drew closer, I could make out the outline of a tall figure leaning against a tree. My pulse quickened.

Rochester was already waiting for me. I picked up the hem of my dress and ran to him. I would have called out, except that I was breathless from trying to bound through the grass in my present costume. Still, I ran. I only wanted to be in my beloved's arms.

Finally within reach, the figure whirled around and launched itself at me. It wasn't Rochester at all, but the madwoman herself. In her rage, she roared unintelligibly and I, too terrified to scream, held up my arms in a futile gesture of protection. The woman tore at my clothing, trying to wrench me apart. Mere inches from my face, her gaping jaw spewed breath that reeked of old blood, ash and decay. Each of her remaining teeth—there wasn't a full set—seemed to be sharpened to a razor's point. She lunged, intent on biting my face with those horrible teeth.

Mercifully, I awoke, drenched in sweat with my arms in the same protective position they'd assumed in my nightmare.

My heart pounded so rapidly, it almost hurt. I tried to take deep breaths to calm down, but the images looped through my mind on a constant instant replay.

I pulled the covers over my head and lay, terrified, as my mind raced. I don't know how long I stayed like that before I was certain I would explode. I considered making some tea to calm myself, but an irrational fear of padding through the dark apartment kept me from pursuing that idea.

I lowered the covers from my head and glanced at my clock. It had advanced to 5:03 am. I abandoned any hope of sleep and grabbed my cell. Turning it on, I was shocked to find twenty texts and ten voicemails, all from Gabriel. It only took looking through a few to see that he was really worried about me and hoped I could forgive him.

Confused, I stopped listening and called him. He answered on the first ring.

"Thank God!" Gabriel's voice came through the earpiece. He sounded dangerously close to tears.

Concern replaced confusion and I pushed myself up. "What's going on?" I demanded.

"I don't know how it happened. One second I was there holding your hand and the next second, I…I'd…" His voice cracked. He was definitely crying.

"What do you mean?" I asked, trying to figure out what he could be referring to.

"I'm so sorry. I can't control it. I just hoped I'd be able to wake you. Are you okay? Please say you're okay."

Slowly, the haze of a memory crept into my brain. I remembered the bizarre street, seeing Gabriel crumple on the porch, the forest.

"You disappeared," I said, finally putting the pieces together. "Are you seriously telling me we were having the same dream together?"

"Oh Christine, I wish that's all it was."

I shook a chill off my spine and stared at the red numbers on my clock. They were real. My bedroom was real. My life was real. Wasn't it?

"How could this happen?" I asked.

"I don't know." His voice sounded so weary to me.

"I stopped asking a long time ago."

"But how can you even function if you're living in a dreamworld all night," I shivered just saying it. "And living a normal life all day?"

"I don't. Not really. That's why I get into trouble. I just react. If it's the dreamworld, there aren't any lasting consequences. If it's the real world, there are."

"But how are you even sane?" I asked.

"Are you sure I am?"

When I didn't answer, he continued.

"Well, if I do have any sanity it's because I write it all down. If I write down what happens, it gives me some power. I can file it away, lock it up in little envelopes to revisit if I choose."

"So why did you let me read any?"

"I don't really know," he admitted. "I just had this crazy compulsion to give you that first one. I thought it was stupid but…" he paused. "I can't explain it."

So many questions jostled my brain, I couldn't think of what to say next. I stared at my clock without really seeing it. Numbness began to settle over me.

"Do you hate me?" Gabriel asked quietly. I jumped, having become so wrapped up in the swirling questions that I'd forgotten he was still on the phone.

"Hate you?" I asked.

"I must have dragged you into this somehow. I disappeared when you needed me. I'm telling you all these crazy things. I'm so sorry, Christine." His voice threatened to break again which wrenched some feeling back into my heart.

"I don't hate you," I said. "I just can't get my mind around this."

The rational choice would be to brand him "crazy" and stay as far away from him as I could. But, clearly, I couldn't do that. Whatever I'd experienced was not within the realm of reason, and he was the only one I had to guide me through it.

I rubbed my forehead and changed my line of questioning.

"So what happened when you disappeared?" I asked. "I mean, what happened here?"

"I just woke up," Gabriel said.

"In your own bed?"

"Yes. Aren't you in your bed?"

"Yes," I answered, drawing my covers up tighter as if they could protect me from the insanity I found myself in.

"I just can't understand this," I said.

"It doesn't make sense," Gabriel replied. "I've spent ten years trying to understand why this happens and I've decided there just isn't an answer."

"There has to be an answer." I realized I was pulling at my blanket so hard the seams were starting to rip. I smoothed it down and took a shaky breath. Gabriel was silent.

"We'll find an answer." My voice came out in a whisper.

More silence.

"Gabriel?"

"I never planned to ruin your life. I only wanted

a chance to be part of it. Now this happened. I'll never forgive myself."

The pain in his voice tugged at my heart. Everything was turned upside down, but I did know one thing. "We're definitely part of each other's lives now. *That* is your fault, but I don't think this…situation is. We'll figure it out. There has to be a way."

"When you say it, I can believe it," he said.

I was glad one of us could.

"Listen," I said. "I gotta get out of here. Daria's in the next room and I don't want to wake her up again."

"Again?"

"Don't ask. Do you want to meet me at the park, under the willow, like last night?" Had it only been a few hours?

"I'll leave right now."

15

Christine

The first faint rays of dawn were breaking over the horizon, breathing life into a new day.

Gabriel was pacing beside his car when I pulled into the parking lot. He rushed right to me as I opened the door.

"Your face!" I exclaimed.

The entire left side of his face was covered in a swollen red bruise that half-closed one of his eyes.

He put his fingertips to his cheek. "I'd forgotten about it. Is it really bad?" He squinted at his faint reflection in my car window and winced. "This'll be fun to explain at work."

"Wait," I said as a cold balloon of dread began to inflate in my stomach. "How do you still have that bruise? I mean…if we were dreaming the whole time…"

Gabriel shrugged. "I don't know how it works. I only know it does a great job of getting me in trouble. You can only claim clumsiness so many times before people start to form their own darker ideas of what's going on."

I clutched my stomach, suddenly gripped by a wave of nausea.

"What's wrong?" Gabriel asked.

I shook my head and closed my eyes, afraid of what would happen if I opened my mouth. Gabriel rested one hand on my shoulder and the nausea passed. I swallowed a few times before attempting to speak.

"After we were in the dreamworld," I started. "I had a nightmare that the madwoman from *Jane Eyre* tried to kill me."

Gabriel clenched his jaw and stared at the trees around the pond.

"Sometimes a dream is still just a dream."

Not knowing what else to do, I started walking toward the willow. I tried to appreciate everything I saw and felt. There must be some sort of difference that would signal the divide between the dreamworld and reality, if there were such a thing.

I listened to Gabriel's footsteps next to mine. At first, they thudded across the concrete of the parking lot and then swished through the grass until we reached the willow. I closed my eyes as I walked under the weeping branches. I didn't move them with my hands; just let them brush my face and catch lightly at my hair. They felt cool and refreshing, even as one of them scratched against my cheek.

Eyes still closed, I leaned against the craggy bark. The pond was not far from the willow and I could hear fish quietly breaking the surface for a gulp of air. I could imagine the tiny bubbles left floating on the surface until they spontaneously popped with a gentle pinprick of sound.

A lone cricket sang his unique song, unanswered by any others.

Secluded within the canopy of the willow, where we'd run into each other not long ago, Gabriel stood close to me. Not close enough to touch, but I could feel the warmth of his body.

The calm of the park and Gabriel's silent presence imbued an illusion of security within me. Our breath fell into rhythm and I noted how my head rose ever so slightly with each inhale.

Having forced myself to sense my surroundings, it occurred to me that no matter where I found myself, simply being a part of it made it real for me. Maybe it didn't need to be more complicated than that.

I opened my eyes and looked at Gabriel. The sun was rising on the horizon, blood red and enormous. The assurance of a new day gave me hope. In the scarlet light, his eyes searched mine, heavy with worry.

"It's gonna be okay," I said.

"What about you?"

I gazed through the branches at the pond. "I feel a lot better here."

"Me too. Let's stay here forever."

I let my eyes roam over Gabriel's face, no longer self-conscious. His eyes betrayed the heaviness of his heart. His battered face was even more swollen.

"We've got to fix you up," I said. "It's getting worse."

Coming back from a million miles away, he startled at my voice.

"Oh, yeah. I keep forgetting."

"How can you possibly forget? Doesn't it hurt?"

He shrugged. "It's not the most painful thing right now."

"Come on," I urged, pushing off from the tree trunk. "You need ice on that."

"I have some at my place," he said.

We stared at each other, letting the realization that he'd just asked me back to his place sink in.

"Then let's go," I answered.

We headed back to the cars. When he started to veer toward his driver's side, I glanced at his face.

"Are you sure you can drive with your eye like that?"

"You're probably right," he said and held his keys out to me. "Do you mind?"

"Not at all," I said.

At least it gave me something concrete to do.

16

Gabriel

Having her in my apartment feels like a premonition. It's an eerie, electric feeling and I still don't feel the pain until she places the washcloth full of ice on my cheek.

"Ooh!" I wince.

"Sorry," she says, and the way her eyelids squeeze together like she's in pain for me makes me long to kiss her again. I restrain myself, though. She's trying to be helpful and it's an exquisite torture to see someone like her help someone like me. I don't deserve it. I don't deserve her. Especially after I've dragged her into this mess. But no. I won't think about that right now.

"It's okay," I say. "I guess it's more tender than I realized."

She shakes her head and I catch the disbelief in her glance. "If you haven't realized this hurts, you're a lucky guy."

I can't help but smile. She just pulls them out of me. It's effortless to be comfortable with her. It's even possible to feel happy.

I see that she's trying to check out my place without

being obvious. Now that we're settled on my bed, the only place to sit, I gently remove her hand from the ice pack and hold it in place myself.

"I never expected a bachelor pad to be so neat," she says.

"When you move around a lot, you learn to travel light."

I see the muscles near her eyes twitch slightly like she's suddenly uncomfortable, but she masks it quickly. She turns away from me to look behind her, at my bookcase of envelopes.

"Are these all your stories?" she asks, running a finger over them.

I nod, even though she's not looking. "That's all of them."

She turns back to me, her eyes wide. "There's so many!"

"Years of dreamworld adventures add up."

Her eyebrows bend together in worry and I feel like I'm being a dick. At the very least, I'm certainly not racking up any points for romance.

"It isn't always bad," I say.

The way she tilts her head is an unasked question. Again I feel the urge to end my pathetic attempt at conversation and just kiss her, but I know she deserves better. I will answer every one of her questions.

I lean over and thumb through the envelopes. I almost know them all by heart. When I've finally come to the one I want, I slide it out and offer it to her. She shakes her head.

"Would you read it to me?" she asks.

The thought of reading this aloud to her makes my pulse go into overdrive. I look up from the envelope for a second and the tremulous expectation on her face is all I need. I will do anything for this girl. No matter what she asks. No matter if she doesn't ask.

I wonder if she's an angel.

My fingers fumble with the lip of the envelope and I slide out the sheet of paper from inside. This is a short one.

I begin to read:

Even in the loneliest existence, one can still find beauty.

I found myself at the end of a long dock over an enormous lake. If I looked ahead or to either side, I could believe I was standing in the middle of an ocean. Ambiguous black terrain surrounded the lake, far in the distance. I imagined that the lake was surrounded by nothing but uninhabited forest. That appeared to be all there was behind me.

I was fortunate to have found myself here at a magical time, sunset. With no sounds other than the gentle water, the sun had begun to paint with beautiful fire in the sky. Against a dark blue background, the sun had splashed deep orange, pink, yellow, purple and red. The colors ran together in some places and all of them melted out of the sky and into the water. As they became darker and more brilliant, I found myself completely surrounded by color and light. The fading sun sparkled on the rippling water and everywhere above and below burst with magnificent color. Had I been placed inside a watercolor painting? I'd stared at so many paintings, trying to find the truth in them; I'd never imagined what it would really be like to experience the world of the painting—just a snapshot in time, tidily framed by a complementary border so that nothing could encroach on the subject.

For the first time in years, I felt safe and peaceful. Grateful for this unexpected taste of tranquility, I hoped that my luck had changed, even though I knew better. At the very least, I knew it didn't always have to be bad.

I return the paper to its envelope before I look at her. She is leaning her chin in her hand and tears shine in her eyes, but they don't spill. Did I do something wrong again?

She removes her hand from her chin and places it on my knee. "It's a beautiful scene," she says softly. "But still so sad."

I shrug. What can I say? It's true but I don't want her to feel sorry for me. I don't deserve any emotion from her, even though I crave it. I may live the life of a freak, but I'm still human. Of course I want her. She's everything I could…She's just everything. Period.

I drop the ice pack and lean close to her. "Guess what?" I ask.

"What?" her voice is barely a whisper.

"You make me happy," I say. I am ready to explode with my desire to kiss her, but she blushes and turns away.

Before I can say anything, she turns back, wide-eyed.

"I have to get to work!"

Shit.

17

Christine

This time, Laura noticed. Forty-five minutes isn't as easy to overlook as fifteen.

"I'm so sorry!" I exclaimed.

Laura raised her hand to stop me. "It's okay. Daria told me. Are you sure you feel good enough to work? You have plenty of sick days if you just want to rest at home. Sometimes it's tough to be a woman." She smiled sympathetically and I tried to act like I knew what she was talking about.

"I'm fine now," I said. "It's probably better to be around people than sit at home dwelling on it."

She nodded, then added, "I've got some Midol in my purse if you need any."

Ah. Daria told her I had cramps.

"Thanks," I said and headed up to the desk.

"Here you are!" Tiffany exclaimed when I finally made my appearance. "You didn't answer any of my texts, you brat!"

Daria subjected me to one of her assessing gazes.

"Nice of you to show up," she said. "Everything all right?"

"Rough night," I said, hoping I wouldn't have to come up with anything else. I'd had enough forethought to leave Daria a note but I'd just told her I couldn't sleep so I'd gone to 7-Eleven.

Tiffany and Daria exchanged glances and, this time, it was more than the pity-face.

I racked my brain for a nugget of normalcy to save me. I practically laughed when I came up with it.

"Fill me in," I said to Tiffany. "How'd it go with Marcel last night?"

Tiffany grinned, but Daria turned away from me. She knew something wasn't right. Tiffany, too eager to notice any weirdness, launched into her tale of love.

"He had these perfectly cut black pants and a silvery blue button-down shirt with a black jacket. It was so hot. American boys don't wear anything classy on a date."

"Sounds awesome," I offered, wondering what Tiffany would think of me and Gabriel standing barefoot in the river.

Our conversation was put on hold as a steady stream of patrons came to the desk. I put on my autopilot smile and stifled the thoughts in the back of my mind. I knew Gabriel was somewhere in the building but I hadn't seen him since he'd dropped me at my car in the park. I'd insisted on going back to the park because there was no way I could explain showing up with Gabriel. Daria would kill me. I hoped he hadn't gotten any flak for the state of his face. I'd tried to cover it up a bit with makeup but it still looked terrible. The ice hadn't done as much for the swelling as I'd hoped.

A stubbly, forty-something man stepped up to the desk with a greasy smile on his face.

"So, Christine," he said, letting his gaze linger on the nametag just above my breast. A sickening pit began to churn in my stomach. "What's a pretty girl like you doing frowning like that? Bad day already?"

I floundered. "Didn't mean to be frowning, just concentrating."

"Got too much on your mind? You should come out for a drink with me. When's your lunch break?"

"I, um, actually have plans for lunch," I said unconvincingly.

His smile got a little wetter. "You have time for a quick drink. I'll meet you in the parking lot and we can head up to your favorite bar. You are old enough to drink, aren't you?"

Sure that my cheeks were purple with embarrassment, I clambered for a surefire answer to get rid of this guy, but it wasn't necessary. The man lurched forward, like he'd been pushed hard. He turned around, eyes bulging in surprise, to find Gabriel behind him.

"Take a hint, she's not interested."

Unfortunately, the man was not as easily persuaded by Gabriel as the crabby lady had been. "Is this your girlfriend or something, punk?"

"Her personal life is none of your business. She's working, not waiting to get picked up by men her father's age."

"I want to see your boss," the man said, jabbing a stubby finger in Gabriel's face.

"With pleasure," said Gabriel. He disappeared into the back to find Laura.

The man turned back to me. "Your boyfriend's a little hot-tempered, honey. You better settle him down."

I had no words. Daria was still helping a patron, but Tiffany was frozen at her computer, gaping at me like a fish on a hook. Still, she recovered first, marched over to me and turned the sign on my desk to "closed." "She's on break," she said, and with a hand on my back, steered me toward the staff area. We passed solemn-faced Laura and Gabriel on their way out.

"Don't go far," Laura said to Tiffany and me.

"She just needs a few minutes to breathe," Tiffany replied. She didn't take her hands off me until we made it into the empty break room. "Are you all right?" she burst out immediately. "What the hell is going on around here?"

Overwhelmed by everything, my eyes welled up and I tried my best to keep them from spilling over. Without missing a beat, Tiffany wrapped me in a hug and I let a few silent tears trail onto her shoulder.

When I finally gained control of my rogue watery eyes, I pulled away and fanned my hot face with my hands. "Well, that was horrible. You'd think by now I could tell a guy to buzz off."

"Obviously, Gabriel can. Anything you need to tell me?" Tiffany crossed her arms over her chest.

There was no way I could lie to her face. Not Tiffany. We'd been friends for too long.

"I ran into him at the park last night," I blurted out.

Her sparkling sapphire eyes almost launched right out of her head.

"You what?"

"Sorry," I said, braced for the fallout.

"Sorry? You better be! And when were you planning to tell me about this little development? Or, let me guess, lost your cell?"

"No, no, of course not. I didn't know if it meant anything and I didn't want to bother you on your date."

"Well, looks like it meant something to him. Enough that he might have just lost his job. I can't believe you didn't tell me!"

I looked at the floor.

"It wasn't my best decision," I mumbled.

"No kidding," Tiffany agreed.

Neither of us said anything for a moment.

I heard her exhale and she uncrossed her arms. "Well, this would be the part where you fill me in."

I would never be able to tell Tiffany about the important things, but I confessed to the stories and him finding me in the park while I was reading and "a" kiss.

Before she could comment, the break room phone rang, which brought us back to the situation at hand. Tiffany answered it. "Yes, we'll be right there."

She hung up the phone and took a deep breath.

"Laura wants to see us."

I rubbed my face. "Why did he do this?"

Tiffany smirked. "A beautiful woman can drive a man to distraction."

"I hope it doesn't drive him to unemployment."

Tiffany shrugged. "Well, I guess it's time to go see."

She linked her arm through mine as we headed out of the break room.

"I never expected you to pick a troublemaker," she whispered.

She wasn't the only one.

18

Gabriel

I watch Christine and Tiffany walk by, arm in arm, on their way into Laura's office. I want to stop Christine and tell her before she goes in, but seeing her with her friend, I lose my nerve. All I do when she meets my eyes is shrug my lips into a guilty smile and wiggle my fingertips in a lame wave. She has worry all over her face, but I can tell she doesn't want to say anything in front of Tiffany.

As they close the door behind them and enter the realm of workplace doom, I am sickened by how I've ruined her life. She can't even talk to me in front of her friends because there's nothing normal to say. I've screwed this up, big time, but all she shows me is kindness. She's an angel. I should leave her alone before I end up turning her into a freak like me.

I get up and head toward the staff copy room. I'm so mad at myself, I just rip off my nametag instead of unpinning it. I shove it into my mailbox as I turn to go.

Is it lucky that Laura didn't fire me on the spot? I'm not so sure. I'm on a three-day suspension, no pay, effective this minute. The only reason she didn't fire me is she does believe I was only trying to protect Christine from that disgusting pervert. She has to suspend me because I didn't do it the right way. If only she knew what I'd really intended to do to him.

Not wanting to go sit in my empty cell of an apartment for the rest of the day, I decide to just drive for a while.

I fling open the doors of the employee entrance and cross the parking lot to my car. Once I get into the driver's seat, the hot air inside is stifling, just like most things in my life.

I turn on some music in an effort to lose what's left of myself in the notes of long-dead composers. My ears are greeted by Ravel's masterpiece, "Bolero." Given the way my heart is pounding, it seems an appropriate choice. I turn it up loud.

I drive and listen. The music makes me feel like a man on a quest, marching, marching, constantly onward. What I'm marching to is unknown. Will it be glory? Will it be a pathetic end? I have my suspicions but there's no way to know until it happens.

The music almost does its job. For a moment, I consider driving off and finding my next life. Maybe I can be strong, for once, and leave Christine in peace. But I think of her eyes, the red highlights in her chestnut hair, the rosy pink of her kissable lips. Just imagining her makes me fidgety and restless, wanting to be next to her again. Oh, there's no way I could do it.

And then I realize what I've done. Oh shit. Why can't I learn to control my impulses? I glance at the clock in the dashboard. It's too late. I've already been driving around for over an hour. She's probably seen it already.

I sigh. No, there's no way I can quietly slip out of Christine's life now. I left her *that* story.

19

Christine

Tiffany and I had explained all we knew to Laura. I'd never seen her so tight-lipped and professional. She wouldn't come out and tell us what had happened to Gabriel, thanks to employee confidentiality, but I just knew he was gone. Whether for the day, the week, forever, I didn't know.

Exhaustion tugged at me but there was no time to rest. There were still patrons to serve. Daria had to share her version of events and then, maybe, I could start the process of forgetting about this day.

Tiffany and I resumed our place at the desk and let Daria go back to talk with Laura.

"You okay?" she asked me before heading back.

"It's been a long day, but yeah," I replied.

Daria sized me up for a moment. "We'll talk," she said before she finally walked away.

"She hates him," I said to myself, but loud enough for Tiffany to hear.

"Nah," said Tiffany. "She doesn't hate him, just thinks he's imbalanced."

"That's basically the same thing," I said. "And you

think he's a troublemaker."

"Can you deny that he's caused more drama here in a few days than in the entire two years we've worked here? I'm not saying it wasn't well-deserved drama, just unusual."

She was right, but I could never explain why he acted the way he did. Troublemaker was a better label than lunatic.

"And since you revealed the park rendezvous bombshell, I do need to ask if you know why his face looked like someone tried to smash it in. You wouldn't have been responsible for the makeup job, would you?"

My cheeks burned. How could I make a reasonable excuse for his face?

"Was the makeup that bad?" I tried to deflect.

"Not if you consider what you had to work with." She held my gaze, daring me to feed her a line of crap. I knew I was already on shaky ground. I couldn't screw up any further.

"I don't know the whole story," I began cautiously, "But I do know there was a misunderstanding that involved the business end of a broomstick."

"That's a heck of a misunderstanding!" Tiffany's eyebrows flew up but her eyes didn't reveal suspicion, only surprise.

"I didn't pry," I said.

Tiffany still stared at me.

"Listen," I said. "I know this doesn't look good, but please trust me. If I thought for a second he was dangerous, that would be the end of it. I don't have delusions of reforming a bad guy, I just think he's had a rough life."

Our sophomore year Literature teacher, Mrs. Leeman, had been hell-bent on single-handedly destroying the myth that good girls could change bad boys. Tiffany and I had rolled our eyes a lot in that class and giggled our way through assignments that dealt with analyzing the "reformation fallacy" in the books we read for class.

Tiffany smirked. "I don't know if Mrs. Leeman would agree with you."

Daria sauntered back to the desk, released from her interrogation.

"How'd it go?" I asked.

"Not bad," she said. "I didn't get a clear picture of what went on since I was helping someone for the whole thing. Is Mr. Impulsive still here?"

"I don't think so. Haven't seen him since we got out of Laura's office," I answered.

"Hmm," was all Daria said.

Between checking out patrons and making chit-chat, we managed to make it through the rest of the shift. I raced back to my mailbox, hoping there'd be some sign of what happened to Gabriel. There was an envelope in my box. I snatched it out and tore right into it, thinking it must be an explanation of what happened. It wasn't what I expected, on several levels:

I stood, alone, before the placid lake. The sun was setting over the water. I couldn't tell where the orange, pink and blue water ended and the orange, pink and blue sky began. Surrounded by such calm and beauty, I felt that I'd come home. Had Athena delivered this Odysseus beyond his struggles at last? It was almost too much to hope. As I gazed into the watercolor sky, I realized the only thing missing was a Penelope. That's where the comparison fell flat. I'd never had a Penelope before my troubles began, how could she be waiting for me at journey's end?

I breathed a heavy sigh and turned away from the water. Eyes cast down, I almost didn't notice the slight shimmer beneath my feet. Even immersed in self-pity, my senses had been trained by years of travel to notice the smallest change in scenery.

When I turned back, the lake and sunset were gone. In their place stood a gray stone house. Its three dreary stories looked more like an institution than a house, yet I understood it to belong to a family. The certainty of this knowledge grew as I heard the happy voices of children float out of the house. They were singing a silly little rhyme. I could practically see them, two girls, twirling around and around their playroom as they sang.

The home was happy now but, with a twisting feeling in my gut, I understood that it wasn't to remain that way for much longer. The particular gray hue of the stones and the angle of the light on the windows clearly spelled tragedy. I'd seen that hue too many times and the light never lied.

I turned away from the house. "Not now," I said out loud, although there was no one around. "I can't bear it."

I became conscious of a new sound, a sound I hadn't

heard before. In the air all around me, a woman sighed. It was as if she were breathing on me, to warm me after a wintry chill.

My eyes fluttered like moth wings and I found myself in bed, where I was supposed to be. The light of a new morning sun began to stretch through the window. I watched as it gently pushed the darkness away, silently gaining dominance over night.

Morning came on as it had forever, but something had changed. I closed my eyes so I could recapture the moment before it slipped away forever. I'd heard things before, like I'd heard the children's voices, even though they were deep in the house. I'd never been surrounded by sound before. It was the woman's sigh that was different. I opened my eyes and a humming energy coursed through my body.

Is there a Penelope after all?

"What's this?" Tiffany asked, plucking the pages from my hand. Of all the times for her to catch me with one of Gabriel's stories, she had to find that one. To her credit, her eyes were on me, not the paper.

"It's from Gabriel," I said. "I thought it might be an explanation of what happened, but it's just a story."

Tiffany glanced at the paper. "Another story?"

"He's prolific," I said.

"Like Javier?" she asked.

"Nobody writes like Javier," Daria said, appearing behind me.

I really needed to stop getting caught in awkward moments in that copy room.

"No, not like Javier," I agreed, carefully plucking the pages back from Tiffany. "He writes short stories. He said he'd bring me one, I guess this is it."

"Said he'd bring you one?" Daria asked, turning on me slowly. "And when did that happen?"

"Uh, yesterday."

"So you've been encouraging this boy?" She sounded more like a mom than my friend.

"There's a lot more to him than what you've seen here."

Daria clenched her jaw. "You mean more than a dangerous personality? Please enlighten me."

I didn't want to fight with Daria. I knew things looked crazy from her perspective, and I could agree, he'd acted recklessly at work twice. But if you knew his secret, it actually made sense. At least, it sort of made sense to me.

"We ran into each other at the park," I said. The story came to me easily enough once I started. "Turns out he lives really close and he loves that park too. We just chatted for a while and talked about his writing. Said he'd bring me a story if I was interested. I said I was. That's all."

Daria looked angry. Tiffany looked a little confused. The story I'd told her was slightly different, but she knew better than to bring that up.

"Listen," said Daria, "You are playing with fire. He may seem like a nice enough guy. He may be writing you pretty stories, but there's something about him that you're better off without, okay?"

"He at least needs a friend," I said.

"I haven't known you to be stupid before," Daria answered. "Don't start now." She turned and walked away without giving me a chance to say anything else. It was actually a relief since I had no comeback.

"Oh dear," said Tiffany. "She's going to make this harder than I thought."

20

Gabriel

I'm sitting at a round maple table with a short vase of pink roses in the middle. A clock tick-tocks loudly to my left. I'm staring out a bay window that's draped in white lace curtains. The window reveals an expanse of lush green grass that slopes down to deep, blue, choppy waters. Heavy clouds hang in the sky, threatening to rain at any moment. I am warm inside the house. It is surprisingly bright and cheerful indoors, which is incongruous with the scene behind the pane of glass.

I know, without a doubt that I'm in the dreamworld again. I also know I've been caught. The voice that comes from behind my left shoulder confirms it.

"Holy shit! Gabriel? What the hell happened to your face?"

I don't move or break my gaze from the threatening storm. I will not answer this stranger. I can feel his malice curling around me like smoke.

"It doesn't matter," he says, striding into my periphery. He leans his hands on the table and bends down for a closer look at my face. Still, I refuse to look at his. One fat drop of water plops on the windowpane. It's coming.

"My God," he says. "It really is you, isn't it? After all these years of planning, I've actually found Gabriel Chase."

This wrong name inexplicably fills me with rage. I leap up, startling him back to a standing position.

"I am not Gabriel *Chase*," I hiss.

I see that he can't be much older than me, even though he's wearing dark sunglasses despite the rain and being indoors. His blond hair screams California pretty boy although his outfit is formal, a white button down shirt and black pants. He's shorter and thinner than me, which is good, because I have the urge to smash his face in.

"Down, boy!" he says, holding his hands up. "This is how you welcome me after you've been lost all these years?"

"You better get the hell away before I make you sorry you found me," I say, clenching my hands into fists. My adrenaline is up. I am invincible.

He laughs, outright throws his head back and laughs. I want to crush his windpipe but his hand tightens around my wrist just as I move toward him. Thunder rumbles overhead.

"Watch it, Chase. You're out of your element here," he says.

"I am not *Chase*," I shake his hand off me. My blood is on fire.

"Don't play dumb with me," he snarls, getting in my face. "You look exactly like your father. There's no denying it."

My father? What is this asshole talking about?

I shove him away from me with all my strength. He should have been knocked to the floor but he only staggers backward a few steps.

His lips curve into a malicious smile.

"Well, Gabriel Nobody, the feeling's mutual."

There's a flash in his hand. Before I can react, I see his knife about to plunge into my body. So this is how it ends? But now I'm staring at the gleam of headlights elongating across the darkness on my ceiling. I jump out of bed and turn on the lights. I'm tearing at my shirt, wondering why it isn't soaked in blood already. All I see is a tiny pinprick of blood on my chest, the only evidence that someone actually tried to kill me. My lungs constrict as the facts seep in and I run to the bathroom for some meds, even though I won't be able to go back to sleep tonight, with or without chemical assistance. There isn't any pill that can fix this.

21

Christine

It was a very dark night but the sky was uncommonly clear. Countless stars and planets twinkled silently above me. I don't think I'd ever been able to see so many stars.

The moon, a pale white sliver, glowed high overhead. A cool breeze blew and rustled the grass in the meadow I stood in. I shivered and instinctively crossed my bare arms to conserve warmth. It may be summer, but once the sun went down it could still get chilly. I wished I'd brought my jacket.

"Who's there?" called a male voice anxiously from somewhere behind me.

I whirled around, startled, but unable to see anyone.

"Who's there?" he called again, sounding a little closer.

I wanted to run, but knew I would make too much noise. As I squinted into the darkness, trying to find an escape route, I realized I had no idea where I was. Footsteps sounded closer to me. I began to discern the figure of a tall, thin man coming toward me.

He stopped a few feet away from me and cocked his head, but it was too dark to make out any of his features. "Well, what do you have to say for yourself?" he asked. "This is private property, you know."

Trying to calm myself, I decided the man wasn't necessarily dangerous. If I was, indeed, on his property, he did deserve an answer. I tried to speak, but my mouth felt so dry I imagined a dust cloud would billow out instead of words. I made a couple scratchy gasps before I could finally whisper, "I'm sorry."

"A woman!" he exclaimed. "What are you doing out here all by yourself in the middle of the night? Are you in trouble?"

The note of worry in his voice relaxed me enough that I could finally speak.

"You scared me, that's all. I didn't know anyone was here. Sorry I'm on your land. If I could see anything, I'd leave."

There was silence from the man for a moment before he answered. "You sure you're all right?"

I sighed, the realization suddenly dawning that my last memory was going to bed. I was in the dream-world again.

"I'm fine. I know this is weird. It isn't a habit of mine to show up in people's yards at night."

"Ah," said the man, a satisfied hint of understanding in his voice. "You're an amateur astronomer, too? This field is the perfect viewing place, and tonight is so amazingly clear I just had to set up my telescope and have a look."

"Yes!" I exclaimed overenthusiastically, glad to have a ready-made excuse for this crazy situation. "I love stargazing! I was just taking an evening stroll and happened to wind up in your field. It is a beautiful night, but I should probably be on my way back—"

"No way!" he interrupted. "Since you're here, you might as well have a look with my telescope. The view is incredible. It's just over there." He gestured toward where I'd first heard him calling but I couldn't make out anything in the darkness. Wherever I was, the city slept at night.

Not knowing what else I could do and relieved to have friendly company, I agreed.

"I'm Leo, by the way," he said as we walked toward his telescope.

"I'm Christine."

"Whoa!" Leo exclaimed, grabbing me. I had almost walked right into the telescope. "Your night vision really is bad. I get used to the dark after a while. You're lucky you found your way here at all."

"You don't know what I had to go through to get here."

"Fair enough," Leo conceded. He hunched over the eyepiece of his telescope and adjusted a few things before he seemed satisfied.

"All right," he said. "Take a look at that!"

I carefully stepped up to the telescope. I had never looked through one before and didn't realize what I'd been missing. He'd trained the telescope on what I assumed was Mars. It was a reddish circle with slight white caps on the top and bottom. I decided to play it vague, just in case.

"Stunning!" I exclaimed, and really meant it.

"Isn't it? It's in the perfect location. I couldn't believe my luck! I don't get a chance to come out here with the telescope much anymore, but I just couldn't help myself this time."

"Why don't you?" I asked before I could think better of it.

"College keeps my free time pretty non-existent. Economics isn't much of a pleasure cruise."

"Economics? I could never do that. Is that what you want to do?"

"Sort of," said Leo. "I've always been a math and science geek. I'd like to do accounting at a big firm somewhere. How about you? What are you studying?"

"Actually, I just finished my junior year of high school. I'm working part-time at my local library. I don't know what I'm going to major in yet, but I know it won't be math. I don't have a head for numbers."

Leo laughed and I smiled, even though we couldn't see each other's faces in the dark. I was enjoying myself with this number-loving astronomer, but I wondered where Gabriel was and if he would show up soon.

"So what college will you go to?" Leo asked.

"EMU," I answered quickly.

"EMU?" asked Leo, sounding confused.

"Eastern Michigan University," I clarified.

"Michigan?" he asked. "What made you decide to go there?"

Now it was my turn to be confused. I knew it wouldn't be cool to ask where we were. At that point, Leo might decide I was certifiable, wandering around by myself in the middle of the night and not knowing where I was. Things could go bad fast. How did Gabriel deal with these messy details?

I floundered on, "I live near Eastern. I'm just taking a little break here."

"Ahhh, just another tourist," Leo said. "Have you been out to Yellowstone yet?"

Yellowstone! How had I ended up on the other side of the country? I shivered, suddenly freezing. All I wanted was to wake up safe and sound in my own state, in my own bed.

I must have become too absorbed by my sudden panic. The next thing I knew, Leo was gently shaking my arm. "Hey, Christine, are you all right? You're not having some kind of attack are you?"

I snapped back to my present situation but couldn't shake the coldness from my bones. "I'm just really cold all of a sudden," I offered through chattering teeth. "I forgot to bring my jacket."

I heard the telltale sound of a zipper and then Leo threw his own jacket over my shoulders. It smelled vaguely of coffee and fabric softener. "Come on," he said clamping an arm around my waist. "Sorry to be so touchy-feely, but I'm going to take you up to the house to warm up. We both know you can't see out here, so please excuse me."

My legs tramped along with him although my

mind was suddenly done with this whole experience. I didn't want to chitchat with Leo anymore. I definitely didn't want him to take me up to the house, but what were my options? Run blindly through his yard and risk running face first into Old Faithful? Yellowstone! What if there were bears and wolves out here? *Wake up! Wake up!* There had to be some way to control this. I tried to concentrate on waking up despite being led quickly through the blackness to a stranger's house. *Wake up! Wake up!* I wanted to scream the words out loud but I couldn't risk it. I was sure everyone's hospitality runs out fast when dealing with a psycho.

I stumbled over something and went down hard. "Ouch!" I yelled as a stinging pain sprang to my right knee.

"Are you okay?" Leo asked. The words echoed in my head, as if Leo were in a tunnel far away, until I couldn't hear anything anymore.

22

Christine

I awoke to my alarm blaring. Rolling over to stop the hideous sound caused my knee to throb. I pulled down the covers and gasped. The knee of my pajama pants was stained with blood. I tried to straighten my leg so I could swing it over the edge of the bed. It stung but didn't feel like anything was seriously wrong.

I successfully limped into the bathroom, pulled down my pants and winced. The blood had adhered the fabric to the wound, and a fresh trickle of blood sprang up when they separated. It was a crappy way to start the day. I couldn't imagine how Gabriel managed it all the time.

I took a quick shower and ran back to my room to call Gabriel before I did anything else.

"Good morning, Beautiful," he answered immediately. It was an unexpectedly sweet greeting, but I couldn't get sucked into romance just yet.

"Did you go anywhere last night?" I asked.

"What happened? Where did you go?" The dreamy flirtation he'd answered the phone with was already long gone.

I related the stargazing with Leo, how everything was cool until I realized I wasn't in Michigan. I was a little embarrassed as I explained my increasing panic as Leo tried to help me to his house and then how I hurt my knee.

"I kept telling myself to wake up," I explained. "And eventually the whole thing with Leo just faded away."

"Did you wake up then?"

I tried to think back. "I guess not or else I would have gotten up to take care of my knee. Do you think getting hurt had anything to do with me snapping out of it?"

"I wish," Gabriel said. "I've willed myself to wake up. I've hurt myself in the hopes that the injury would wake me up. I've tried going to sleep there, and that's just a few. I never get out until it's done with me."

"There's got to be something," I said, feeling like my mind was just a drop in an immense ocean of ideas.

"Let me know when you find out," Gabriel said without optimism.

"You know," he continued. "I'm glad someone wanted to help you, especially since I wasn't there for you..." His voice trailed off.

"Forget about it. You can't control what happens there. I know you're here for me."

"Here, yes. I want to be *there* for you, too."

Suddenly, I remembered what had happened pre-dreamworld.

"Hey," I said. "About that, are you going to be 'here'

for me at work anymore?"

"Sorry," he said, "I meant to call you but I sort of felt like an ass and then I left you that story. I guess I made a mess of everything."

"One thing at a time," I said. "First, what happened with Laura?"

"I told her I'd been out of line but that you remind me of my sister and I wouldn't want some creep hitting on her, so I stepped up. Because she appreciated my willingness to protect the staff, but not the way I did it, Laura suspended me for three days."

I breathed a sigh of relief but something stuck in my mind.

"Do you have a sister?" I asked.

"Yes, but you don't actually remind me of her. I mean, you don't look alike but you seem to get me like she does. She's from Guatemala."

"Guatemala?" I repeated, like an idiot.

"Yeah, she's adopted. We both were."

"Oh," I said. It surprised me that Gabriel was adopted and had a sister from another part of the continent. I supposed a lot of things would surprise me because we really didn't know much about each other.

"What's her name?"

"Carmen," he said with a note of sadness in his voice.

"Does she live around here?"

"No. I, uh, actually... I haven't talked to her in awhile."

I felt like crap. Maybe she was dead? Maybe they

didn't get along? It wasn't my business.

"I'm sorry, I shouldn't have—"

"No, you're fine. I'm just not used to talking about my family. Until you, there hasn't been anyone I could talk to."

I felt the saliva beginning to dry in my mouth.

"Do you…" I didn't even know what I wanted to ask, just that the conversation required me to say something. Luckily, he saved me from my own inadequacy.

"Carmen and I were really close, right from the start. I was five when my parents brought her home. She was this beautiful little person and she smiled the first time she saw me. How could I help but love her back?"

"That's so sweet," I said. "I always wished I had a sister."

"We had a lot of fun together, that's for sure. I would've done anything for her. Then, out of the blue, I started going to the dreamworld. I never said anything to Carmen because I didn't want to scare her. I couldn't tell my parents because it was an unbelievable story. If it were true, who would be able to believe it? If it wasn't real, that meant I was insane. It was too terrifying to say out loud."

"How could you stand it?" I gasped.

"The first few years, it wasn't so hard to keep the secret. I didn't go to the dreamworld all that often, maybe a couple times a year. It was pretty neutral stuff then too, visiting zoos with all sorts of animals I'd never imagined before, floating on a rowboat in the middle

112

of the ocean. It wasn't until I turned twelve that things started to get weird. I started encountering people, and none of them seemed to like me. I'd pop up in places I shouldn't be, like when we were in the dreamworld together.

"I started missing school because I'd be so tired in the morning. My parents thought I was sick, so they took me to several doctors. Of course, none of them could find the source of my problems but it didn't stop them from prescribing all sorts of different sleep aids and energy pills."

My mind boggled at the idea of Gabriel, drugged up for a symptom no drug could touch. What was I doing when I was twelve? Tiffany and I were reading books like *Anne of Green Gables* and dreaming about how beautiful our lives would turn out. It seemed ludicrous compared to Gabriel's reality.

"What did you do?" I asked, struggling to keep my voice from shaking.

"I pretty much kept to myself at school. I didn't have the same interests as my friends anymore so they got tired of me. Friendship turned to bullying so I started getting into fights. My teachers suspected drug use because of all the changes, so I had to go to a counselor. I couldn't tell her what was going on, either, so I got labeled a 'difficult' case.

"When I turned sixteen and things weren't improving at all, I decided to run away. I could literally see my parents aging before my eyes because they were so exhausted trying to help me. It was hardest to leave

Carmen but I knew it would best if she wasn't associated with me anymore. It hurt her enough that I wouldn't even tell her what was going on. I didn't want to leave but I couldn't play the game anymore.

"I hurt the only people who mattered to me and I never wanted to do that again," he paused and drew a shaky breath. "But then, I saw you."

My heart beat ferociously.

"You make me care again," he said quietly.

I didn't know what to say. I thought about the last story he had given me. Any suspicions I'd had about the Penelope implications were obvious now. It hit me with certainty: Gabriel was asking me to love him.

In that moment, I knew I should say that I did. It was the only right response, but was it true? We shared an enormous and insane secret but didn't know much about each other. There was no denying the connection between us. But it wasn't a word I could throw around. I just wasn't ready.

"Thank you for telling me," I said, feeling like the world's biggest jerk.

"Are you okay?" he asked, concern returning to his voice.

"I'm fine. It just breaks my heart that you had to go through all that. I wish I could do something to fix it."

"Don't worry about that," he said. "It's enough that you care."

I looked down at the raw, red skin on my knee and knew caring would never be enough.

23

Christine

By now, everyone knew that Gabriel was suspended and that it was because of me. I felt like I couldn't walk anywhere in the library without being followed by whispers. I swear, even the books were whispering about me.

Daria had insisted on driving in with me since our shifts were identical that day. The look on her face had been unreadable but it was better than arguing, or the silent treatment, which is what we'd both been doing since the latest library incident. The ride in wasn't very enlightening. She'd tuned the radio to the contemporary rock station to fill the silence.

But I think it was the whispers at work that broke her down. Perhaps the fact that Tiffany, Daria and I were whispering our way around each other rather than talking like normal. Gabriel's absence permeated the air like the unacknowledged elephant in the room. It meant different things to each of us, but we all knew it was big. Not even Tiffany had the heart for our usual banter.

After an uncharacteristically subdued desk shift,

we were ready to leave. I'd just slammed my locker shut after retrieving my purse when Daria put her hand on my shoulder.

"We are not doing this anymore," she said.

"What?" I asked.

She gestured between her, Tiffany and me. "The weirdness. I'm sick of it."

"Oh, thank God!" exclaimed Tiffany. "I was wondering how long we'd have to be all serious and quiet."

"You," Daria said, pointing at me. "You haven't done a bit of apartment searching, have you?"

I bit my lip.

"I thought not," she answered. "So here's what we're going to do. Our boys can handle their own business for tonight. We're going to spend some girl time together and see if we can find you a place for next year."

No one was going to disagree with her. Frankly, I thought it was a great plan.

"I'll just text Marcel right now, and my parents, and then the phone's going on silent," Tiffany said eagerly.

"I should let Gabriel know," I said, staring straight at Daria. Her jaw tightened but finally, I knew what to say.

"Listen," I said. "It isn't my place to go into details, but Gabriel has a really messed up family life. That's why he acts the way he does, but he isn't a bad person. If you could just stop judging him long enough to see who he really is, you'd know that."

We walked out into the parking lot, Daria carefully

considering what I'd just said.

"I don't think he's a bad person," Tiffany piped up after the silence had become too much for her.

Daria shook her head. "It's not that I think he's a bad person," she said. "But he has a way of attracting trouble. That's what worries me."

"So, he needs to be shunned because, through no fault of his own, he gets into bad situations?" I asked.

"It can't all be coincidence," Daria said gently. We got into her car and she pulled out of her parking space. Before I could protest, she continued. "You have to admit, he didn't need to tell off that old lady. Just like he didn't have to get up in that nasty guy's business."

"But he was—"

"Yes, he was only trying to protect you, but did he have to do it that way? There were other options, Christine. Far less troublesome options."

Daria was right, but I had to make her understand. I didn't want to see that disapproving face of hers for the rest of the summer. Especially if it was the last summer I'd see it.

Finally, Tiffany interjected. "I think you both need to stop. He obviously cares about Christine and she feels the same about him. They're together now. You need to stop arguing about it. Please!"

"I don't want to sit by and watch my friend get hurt." Daria said. She was weakening. I could tell.

"She will or she won't," Tiffany said. "It has to play itself out. So let's not worry about what hasn't happened and worry about getting Christine an apartment instead."

"I like that idea," I said.

"Well, he better not pull any more crazy stunts at work. If he can stop going psycho on the patrons, I'll pretend that never happened. That's the best I can promise." Daria said.

I could have hugged her. "Sounds fair to me."

We made it to Daria's and sat on the floor in the living room. Daria grabbed her laptop and loaded the page for the EMU newspaper. "We'll start with the classified ads in this," she said. "People are always looking for roommates and people to sublet. We can make a list of the most promising ones and then make some phone calls."

"This is so exciting!" exclaimed Tiffany. "Do you really think you can get your parents on board?"

"Well, I need to think of every angle. Make it as hard as possible for them to say no." My mom was already pretty weak on the subject. She really felt terrible about me starting a new school for senior year. Dad was more resistant. Either way, I had to try. There was too much going on in Michigan for me to leave now.

24

Christine

So many stars shone overhead that I could see our arm of the Milky Way extending from beyond Earth and into the vastness of space. I raised my arms to the sky, letting the universe wash over me. It was so dark it was easy to imagine I was floating in space, not unlike another wonderful evening I'd had. If I hadn't been so absorbed by the beauty around me, I might have realized where I was.

"I wondered if you'd be back."

I gasped and whirled around to find the source of the vaguely familiar male voice. I felt like I was in a bad movie where the main character is searching for something and the camera darts around wildly, trying to capture the object of the actor's desire or dread.

"Who...?" is all I managed to say before he spoke again.

"Ouch! I thought I was at least a little memorable."

Finally, I could make out the silhouette of a tall, thin man slowly walking toward me. A strong sense of déjà vu jarred my memory.

"Leo!" I exclaimed as relief flooded through me.

"I'm sorry, I didn't realize I was back in your field."

"Do you want something from me?" he asked, sounding anxious and excited at the same time.

"Do I want something?" I asked, not understanding. "Why would I want something from you?"

"You tell me," he answered.

I shrugged into the darkness. "I'm afraid I don't understand."

"Maybe you don't, but I do." Leo said, but not in a threatening way.

More intrigued than startled, I wanted to know more. "Could you enlighten me?" I asked.

There was silence for a moment before I heard a deep breath. "You…well…you aren't from here."

"No," I said cautiously.

My caution seemed to embolden him a bit. "Then there's the small matter that you disappeared into thin air last time."

I'd been so relieved to find myself with Leo again instead of somewhere horrible that I'd completely forgotten what had happened before. Maybe this wasn't going to be a safe haven after all.

"I'm sorry for that," I said. "I don't even know how to explain."

"Somnium conciliator?" he asked. It sounded like a question, although he said it so quietly and it didn't make any sense.

"What was that?" I asked.

"But it's obvious," he went on in a regular voice. "Something very unusual is happening here."

"That's an understatement," I said.

"I also have a suspicion that we both know more than we're letting on."

His suggestion prompted a feeling of relief, even though the implications should have scared me.

"That's a distinct possibility," I replied, hoping that Leo did know something that could help.

"But how can I trust that you'd tell me the truth?" he continued.

He had a point there, especially since I was the one who'd disappeared the last time we met. I didn't know why, but I felt an overwhelming compulsion to tell Leo everything. Something about Leo seemed safe. He was a mostly anonymous guy in Wyoming who enjoyed stargazing and mathematical equations. He would never be able to expose my secret, and once I disappeared tonight, there was no telling if I'd see him again.

"Well, I guess there isn't anything I can do to make you trust me, but I'd like to tell someone the truth. It'll sound insane, but if you're up for it, I feel like I can trust you."

Leo considered this briefly. "Well, if you trust me, I'll trust you."

"Okay," I said. "But we should probably sit down for this."

"Do you want to sit on my porch?"

The prospect of getting it all off my chest made going up to the house a lot less creepy than it had seemed the last time.

"Perfect, except I can't see a thing in this darkness."

"Night vision isn't one of your secrets, huh?" Leo said with a hint of playfulness.

"No, it's a common misperception that people who disappear into the night can, in fact, see at night."

"Well, since I remember what happened to you last time, take my arm so I can lead you up to the house, unless you'd rather freak out."

"Very funny," I said humorlessly. "Once you hear what I've been dealing with, you'll understand that I have a right to freak out." I walked over to his silhouette and linked my arm with his. It was much thinner than Gabriel's but it was still comforting. I didn't need to go home with another gash on my leg.

The house was farther away than I expected. The porch light was on, so once he pointed it out, I could see where we were headed. I was still grateful for Leo's steady arm to help me navigate the unfamiliar terrain.

There was a wooden bench swing on the porch, like an old couple would have, but I wasn't in a position to criticize. Once we got settled on the swing, I turned to look at Leo for the first time. He had straight blonde hair pulled into a ponytail, gold wire glasses, a sharp nose that reminded me of a hawk, and a soft, friendly mouth. He was even thinner than I'd suspected, but he didn't look sickly. He was wearing a green flannel shirt and faded jeans with black All-Star sneakers.

"It's nice to finally see you," I said.

He smiled, revealing endearingly crooked teeth, not so bad that he should have had braces. They were simply normal, something I was beginning to value greatly.

"Nice to see you too, Christine." He stared at me, looking expectant.

I suddenly felt shy and looked down at my hands rather than face Leo. The overpowering urge to share this secret with someone had faded into feeling ludicrous. Could I really expect anyone to believe the truth?

"I'm waiting," Leo reminded me softly.

The gentleness in his voice was all I needed to take a deep breath and plunge in. I told him everything, from meeting Gabriel that first day, to my first solo visit to the dreamworld, right up to that moment on the swing. I spilled every little detail I could remember, and when I was done, I slowly turned my eyes to Leo to gauge his reaction. He was silently gazing up into the stars. After several minutes, I couldn't stand it anymore.

"I'm waiting," I reminded him, using his own words.

Without breaking his gaze from the heavens, he furrowed his brow. "I've never heard of anything like this before."

"It sounds really stupid," I started, but he shook his head and turned to pierce me with those blue eyes of his.

"No," he said firmly. "I believe you, I just can't figure out how it's possible."

"Me neither!" I agreed, the weight of the whole crazy secret starting to float away. "The absurdity is that back in Michigan, my body is sleeping in my bed and when it chooses to wake up, I will disappear from your reality completely and be back in my real world. It doesn't make any sense at all, but that's the truth."

Leo stood up and started pacing in front of the swing. He shoved his hands into his pockets and went back to stargazing as he paced.

"So you can't leave here of your own free will?" he asked.

"I haven't been able to yet, and neither has Gabriel, and he's been dealing with this a lot longer than me. I can't come here when I want either, so this is, theoretically, the last time I'll see you."

"There's got to be something we're missing," he mused.

I liked the way Leo's mind worked. The wheels were turning, straining to make sense of this crazy puzzle, and he didn't even think I was nuts. I felt a surge of hope that if anyone could unravel the mystery, it was Leo, and I needed to believe there was a way we could contact each other.

"You'd really be willing to help me?" I asked.

"Clearly, somebody needs to." He smirked, but in the way friends do when they're teasing.

"But, I think, before we go any further," he continued. "You need to be able to contact me."

I closed my eyes, fully expecting to wake up in my bed simply because I wanted to stay so badly.

"Hang on until I get back," Leo said. I heard a bang and opened my eyes. Leo wasn't on the porch anymore. It took a moment to realize he'd run inside and the bang had been the screen door. I began to feel like a predictably scripted horror movie. "Leo, hurry!" I yelled. I don't know why, but I suddenly knew without a doubt that I was about to leave. I couldn't pinpoint the exact difference, but I felt like Wyoming was becoming blurry around the edges, like waking up from a dream. For the first time, I fought to hang on. "Leo, I'm going! I can't help it!"

"Don't!" he yelled. I heard the surreal echo of the door bang again, and then I was gone.

I grudgingly opened my eyes, unprepared for the rage I felt when I saw the glowing 3:18 am on my alarm clock. Before I could think, I snatched the clock and hurled it against the wall.

Daria was in my room in an instant.

"What's wrong?" she asked, panic thick in her voice.

"Another nightmare," I said, annoyed with myself for waking her up.

Daria was silent for a few moments. When she spoke, her voice was quiet and had a tone of uncertainty that Daria normally didn't have.

"I'm worried about you. Maybe you need to talk to someone."

I almost laughed. She thought a therapist could help me out of this mess. If only.

"There's nothing wrong with asking for help," she continued. "You're facing a huge transition. You're getting involved with the wrong kind of guy. It's a lot to take."

"Would you leave Gabriel out of it?"

"No, I won't. You've changed since he showed up. You're secretive, showing up later for work, having these nightmares. Getting involved with him isn't doing you any favors. I wish you'd see that."

My words had to be chosen with care.

"I thought you agreed to give him another chance, or does that not apply in the middle of the night? You have to believe that I know what I'm doing."

"Mm hmm," Daria replied. "Is that why you're smashing stuff against the wall in the middle of the night?"

There was nothing I could say.

Daria turned to go, but she stopped in the doorway.

"I know you're upset with everything," she said. "But if this keeps up, maybe you should find another place to stay for the rest of the summer." After dropping this bombshell, she padded back into her bedroom and shut the door.

Another place to stay. That's exactly what I was trying to do. She'd just helped me make some calls, which hadn't gone so well. She knew as well as I did that nobody was particularly interested in having a minor move in. We'd called at least a dozen places and I was no closer to finding a place than before.

I stared into the darkness until the dull light of dawn softened the black into gray. My thoughts tumbled over and around each other until my mind felt like a tangled mess. As the room continued to get lighter, my eyes focused on the severely cracked clock and the fine dent it had left in the wall. Something else lay crumpled on the floor about halfway between the clock and my bed. I leaned forward to retrieve it and realized it was a dollar bill. Smoothing it between my fingers, I noticed writing on it. I stopped short when I saw a phone number with a name beneath: *Leo.* My heart throbbed in my chest. There must be thousands of Leos in the world with their phone numbers scrawled on dollar bills. Surely, this was a cruel coincidence.

The numbers whirled around in my brain, buzzing with possibility. There was one easy way to find out if this was what I hoped it was, but I couldn't dare to do anything unless I was sure.

I quickly did a search on my phone for area code 307. I held my breath as the results appeared on the screen. *Area code 307 is in Wyoming,* it read. I tried to believe that it could still be a coincidence, but hope was already flooding into my body. If this was real, could helping Gabriel be as easy as a phone call? It seemed crazy enough to be possible, but I was terrified to dial the number. Too much was riding on a potential breakthrough of this magnitude.

I knew I had to make a phone call right away, but it wasn't to Wyoming. I wasn't ready to try that yet. Instead, I called Gabriel and told him everything. There was a long pause after I'd relayed the events of my evening to him.

"So, what you're telling me," Gabriel started slowly, "is that you traveled to the dreamworld and got some guy in Wyoming to give you his number."

"This is not the time to be jealous," I said.

"I know. It's just my lame attempt to be casual about the most horrifying news you could have told me."

"I know what you mean. So what should I do? I was too scared to call the number, but what if Leo can really help?"

"Yes, we definitely have to call him, but will you wait for me to come over first? I don't want you to be by yourself to do something so crazy, especially since it's my fault."

"You have to stop saying that," I reminded him. "And I think it'd be better if I came to your place."

"Whatever you want."

25

Gabriel

My thoughts are a photomontage in fast forward. I see flashes of everything I've ever seen in the dreamworld. I see Christine's eyes. I even see the yellow glow of hope seeping into my vision. It's also tinted by a stronger glow, green jealousy. I can admit I'm threatened by this Leo guy. How could I not be?

The guy trying to kill me isn't enough now. It has to go one step further and steal my girl. I truly am the most cursed person alive.

Should I even tell her what happened last night? While the smooth operator was escorting her through dreamland, psycho killer came back for me. I squeeze my eyes shut to push back the memories, but nothing can keep them out.

I can't tell her that. It's too much. There has to be a "normal" somewhere. Normal does not involve a guy trying to shank your boyfriend in his dreams.

A strong, sickening feeling expands my guts. Cold sweat covers the back of my neck. I make myself sick these days. I can't keep something this real and horrible from her but she doesn't deserve to have what's left of her life stolen by my problems.

I run to the bathroom to splash cold water on my face. The icy drops bring me back from the brink of panic. I stare at my reflection in the mirror. All I see is fear looking back. I don't know if I can afford not to tell her but I just don't know how I can.

26

Christine

And where do you possibly need to go at three o'clock in the morning?"

I spun away from the front door to face Daria's silhouette. Caught in the act. It probably wasn't the smartest idea to leave so soon after the alarm clock incident, but what could I do? Gabriel and I needed to talk things out. We needed to figure out if I really had Leo's phone number in my pocket. But what could I possibly tell her?

"Don't bother feeding me a line of crap, Christine. You need to tell me the whole truth, right now."

I sighed. The whole truth wasn't an option, but I knew there was no use lying about believable things.

"I need to see Gabriel," I said.

Daria crossed her arms. "Is that so?"

"It's complicated."

"Oh, I'm sure it is. Let me make it easy on you. You're not going."

How was this happening?

"Come on, Daria. You sound like my mom."

"Great idea!" Daria exclaimed with mock

cheerfulness. "How about this? If you leave this apartment tonight, I'm calling your mom."

I snorted and threw my arms in the air. "After all these years, how can you not trust me? The guy *protected* me at work. Twice! Believe me, he's not trying to hurt me. You, on the other hand…"

"This isn't like you. All the red flags are there—"

"Spare me your 'red flags.' You took a couple psychology classes and now you're an expert in my life? I thought you knew me better than this."

"So did I," Daria scoffed. "But I'm guessing you never went to 7-Eleven that morning when Gabriel showed up with his face all busted up. Oh, let me guess, he ran into a door, right?"

It was getting difficult to control the volume of my voice. "It's none of your business what happened to his face."

"Of course not," Daria continued, smooth as ever. "And it shouldn't bother me that one of my best friends is hanging around with a guy who gets beat up in the middle of the night and tries to start fights with people at work."

"You don't know anything about him."

"And what do you know? You haven't known him any longer than I have. Would you just stop a minute and look at yourself?"

I took a deep breath in an effort to calm down.

"It looks bad. All right? I know that. But it honestly isn't what it seems. You have to trust that I know what I'm doing. Can you please do that?"

Daria crossed her arms. "Not at three in the morning, I can't."

I covered my face in my hands. I loved Daria, but sometimes, she could be too stubborn.

"Can we come up with a compromise that doesn't involve you kicking me out or calling my parents?" I relented.

"That's up to you."

I threw my hands up. "I don't want to argue with you. I don't want to make you mad."

Daria sighed. "All right. Can we agree that three in the morning isn't the best time to go visiting?"

"Yes." She had me there.

"If you go back to bed and wait, at least until the sun rises, I'd feel a whole lot better about the situation."

My body was straining to move out the door and talk to Gabriel about calling Leo, but I couldn't go against Daria. Not with the position I was in. If my parents made me come to Texas now, I wouldn't have a chance at anything. Especially not helping Gabriel.

"Okay, but I have a condition of my own," I said.

"What's that?" Daria asked, unable to contain the slight edge in her voice.

"You really have to stop acting like Gabriel is a criminal. He's my friend now. I'd appreciate if you could respect that."

"I don't want that *friend* in my apartment. And if he can pull himself together to start acting like a normal part of society, I'll rethink my position. That's the best I can do."

For Daria, that was a pretty big deal.

"Okay," I said, heading back toward my room. "That's good enough for me."

"Don't make me regret this," Daria mumbled.

Once I'd closed my bedroom, I grabbed my cell and sent Gabriel a quick text.

Can't come after all. Be there around 7 instead. Goodnight.

Then I turned off my phone and got back into bed. I had no intention of trying to sleep. There was no chance of that happening anyway. But staring at the ceiling was the only way I could think to pass the remaining hours until Gabriel and I could get some answers.

27

Christine

At exactly 7:05 am, Gabriel and I sat shoulder to shoulder on the floor of his apartment with the phone in front of us. Daria hadn't come out of her room when I left, but I knew she was up. I felt bad, but she just couldn't understand. I'd had to go.

Gabriel kept fidgeting with his hands, crossing his arms, drumming his knees with his fingers, crossing his arms again. I had already tried seven times to make the call, but I couldn't go through with it. As much as I wanted to know if communicating with Leo would be as simple as a phone call, it was also terrifying to imagine. If this worked, then I had really met a guy in a Wyoming field, even though I'd never officially gone to Wyoming in my life. Visiting a dreamworld was a freaky thought, but at least I could assume what went on there wasn't real. This dollar bill had drastically changed the game.

Finally, I took a shaky breath. "I'm really going to do it now."

Gabriel gave a quick nod and crossed his arms again. "You don't have to call if you don't want to."

"No," I said, picking up the phone. "I'll go insane if I keep wondering about it. It's gotta be now." I dialed the numbers as I spoke.

Gabriel tentatively reached out and squeezed my knee. "I'm right here with you."

As the phone rang, sweat prickled under my arms and I was seized with a feeling of suffocation. Just as I was about to hang up, the ringing stopped and a familiar voice greeted me.

"Hello?"

My voice completely failed me.

"Hello? Is this Christine?" he asked. Apparently, Leo was always going to be one step ahead of me.

"I," was all I managed to choke out.

"What took you so long? I was afraid you hadn't found the dollar. Do you know how worried I was that you'd never call?"

"Leo," I said.

"Yes?"

"I'm kinda freaking out right now."

"What's wrong?"

"Well, for starters, I'm talking to you on my phone. This is pretty much the most frightening phone call I've ever made."

"No, no," said Leo. "Relax. This is good. It's the only way I can help you."

"Do you have any ideas?" I asked, clutching the phone like it was a life preserver in a stormy ocean.

Leo inhaled deeply. "Christine, what if I told you things aren't quite what they seem, including me?"

His words chilled me until I actually shivered. Gabriel ducked his face down to search my own. There was no masking his concern.

Holding his gaze, I slowly answered Leo.

"I'd say I'm not entirely surprised, but tell me what you're talking about."

I heard some kind of shuffling on Leo's end and a heavy sigh.

"This is harder than I thought," he said. "I was sworn to secrecy about all this..."

"Just summarize, in a general way. I don't need any more secrets."

Leo sighed again. "Okay, here's the thing. I'm not really studying economics right now. I was going to, so don't think I outright lied to you. But, I have a job."

The way he said "job" made it sound suspicious.

"Okay," I prompted, wary of learning someone else's secret.

"I work in a top-secret government agency. I know that probably sounds insane, but it's the truth.

"What I want you to know is that Gabriel is a highly coveted missing person for us. His father was a very influential, high-ranking official in our division until he was murdered. We've been searching for Gabriel ever since because we have reason to believe he's inherited, if not surpassed, the natural abilities of his father. So far, he's proven to be an incredibly elusive target.

"Are you still with me?"

In truth, my brain went numb at "top secret

government agency," but I had to let him go on.

"Yes," I confirmed in a dry voice.

"Okay, if I brought Gabriel back to the agency, I would be a hero. One of our main objectives has been to find him and we'd all die for the chance to be the one to do it. But there's one huge problem."

"And that is?"

"You."

My fingers clutched the phone in a death grip, hoping that Gabriel wasn't able to hear anything Leo was saying.

"Let me explain that," he continued when I didn't respond. "You are not a problem. The problem, for me, is there's no explanation for you. In my line of work, you don't accidentally bump into someone. The people we deal with have been summoned, but you weren't. Not the first time we met, anyway. So this puts me in a very surreal situation."

"You too, huh?" I asked with no humor in my voice.

"I'm sorry, I don't mean to sound callous. I know you're trying to figure this out, and that's what causes my problem. If I reveal Gabriel, my...let's just say my work...will be traced. That will expose you, too. My superiors aren't going to want to let you walk away."

"Where exactly is the problem for you?" Fear spurred bitchiness.

"The problem is it's clear to me you've been sucked into this whole thing by someone and you should be free to live your life. If you're revealed, that won't be possible. Not naturally, anyway. I couldn't bear to see that happen."

"Why not?" I couldn't really understand everything Leo was telling me, but if Gabriel was such an amazing prize, I didn't see why Leo would let me stand in his way.

Gabriel began drumming furiously on his legs. I reached out to still him. Between his nervousness and the insane things Leo was saying, I was in real danger of losing it.

"Because you trusted me to help you," Leo answered.

My face had been so tense throughout the conversation I was beginning to register the discomfort of a headache.

"So, where does that leave us?" I asked.

"Truthfully," said Leo. "I don't know."

"Fair enough," I said.

"No," said Leo. "None of this is fair. Not to you."

"It's a little late to go back now."

"But I don't have to make things worse," Leo replied.

Neither of us said anything for a minute. My eyes were fixed so intensely on a little patch of carpet in front of me I'm surprised it didn't burst into flame. My brain didn't know where to begin to comprehend what Leo had just told me. I had more questions and fears than ever, so I did the only thing I could. I diverted to something else.

"Do you want to talk to him?" I asked Leo.

"You mean Gabriel?"

"Yes. He's right here."

"Oh, man!" exclaimed Leo. "I wasn't expecting that."

"Yeah, I thought it would be too freaky to call a guy from my dreams by myself. So, do you want to talk to him? Sounds like you have plenty to discuss."

I was about to hand the phone to Gabriel, but Leo stopped me with a forceful, "No!"

"But isn't that your mission?"

"Our mission, yes. I don't know what my mission is anymore. I need to sort that out on my own, but thanks for the offer."

"Okay, well, I guess I'd better go—"

"Wait!" Leo interrupted me. "Obviously, if we met it's possible you could meet other agents. Don't tell anyone else about Gabriel, okay? For your own safety. Promise me."

The hairs on my neck prickled at the mention of my "safety." I didn't need any persuasion.

"I promise."

"Thank you. I've got your number now, so I'll call when I have more information for you."

"Okay," I said.

"And if there's anything I can do to help you or if you have more questions, please call me. I know everything I just said is beyond belief, but I do want to help you. I hope you can still trust me."

"Thank you," I said. At that point, I was so confused I didn't think I could even trust myself.

"Take care, Christine."

"You too," I replied, and then I was just clutching a phone with no connection.

28

Gabriel

She opens her hand, suddenly, and drops the phone on the floor.

"That was intense," she says.

"What happened?" I ask, hoping my voice doesn't betray the edginess I feel. The last thing I want is for her to feel like I'm demanding something from her. She's already given me so much more than I deserve.

She turns to face me. All I want to do is hold her and forget all this craziness, but her face is so serious, the confusion and fear accent her features. The effect is like a dismal mask of the Christine I met that first day. Knowing that it's solely me who has caused her to look like this makes my body feel like a hive of angry bees.

"I guess..." she says quietly. "I guess you're wanted by a secret government agency." As she says the words, her eyebrows raise slightly, as if they hope the whole thing will turn out to be a joke.

I thought I was a hive of bees. Now I think it's killer hornets.

I'm not surprised to hear I'm a wanted man. I've felt like one for years. The reaction coursing through my body comes from the sudden question of whether this "harmless" guy in a field, giving his number to Christine, might be the same guy who's trying to kill me.

"What does Leo look like?" I ask. It doesn't matter what else was said, not if a psycho is toying with her.

Her beautiful blue eyes become pools of questions for a moment before the hardness settles her features again.

Her bottom lip pouts out as she thinks back. I wish I was kissing that lip instead of having this conversation.

"Well, he's taller than me, really skinny but not in a sickly way. He has long blonde hair, glasses and a nose like a hawk."

The killer hornets downgrade back to bees. I relax my hands, which I now realize I've been clenching. She notices.

"Who did you think he was?" she asks.

I think the question catches us both off guard. I don't think she meant to ask it and I still don't know how to tell her.

"I don't know," I say. "What else did Leo tell you?"

Her eyes dart away for a moment; like she also knows something she doesn't want to tell. But all of this is my burden to bear. I have to help her give it over.

I reach out my hand to her and she takes it. Being permitted to just hold her hand calms me.

"You can say anything," I reassure her. "It's all right."

I can see that she still doesn't want to. I try not to

imagine what could be so awful.

"It's your father," she blurts out. "Apparently he was some amazing official in this secret agency but he was murdered and everyone has been trying to find you ever since. They think you might have the same kind of abilities as him. I don't really know what he was talking about; he said he was sworn to secrecy about all of it anyway, but it would be a tremendous honor if he could bring you back to the agency, only he doesn't know what to do because he doesn't know why I'm in the dreamworld. I guess to figure that out he'd have to bring me with you, but he doesn't want to do that either so until he decides what to do, I guess we're both still stuck."

I am not prepared for this. My mind is stuck on two words, father and murdered. My father? *My* father? The only father I have is Joseph Gray and he's home with his wife, Marissa, and my sister, Carmen. I don't know how long it's been since I've talked to them, but surely he can't be—

I think the air is being vacuumed out of my lungs.

Christine squeezes my hand.

I breathe.

I anchor myself to the worry in her eyes.

A thought explodes in my mind. The guy who's trying to kill me said, "I've actually found Gabriel *Chase.*" Now it all makes sense! Someone really is looking for me. Joseph Gray is fine. Chase is my biological father, the man I had quickly imagined away as a deadbeat, one-night-stand kind of guy, but that can't be true, can it? This agency, whatever it is, wouldn't be looking for Chase's son if he, I mean I, was a one-night-stand baby. But why is that guy trying to kill me and why is Leo trying to help Christine? Christine!

I push aside the maddening thoughts and focus on Christine, right here in front of me. She is watching my mind self-destruct with a quiet reverence. She is so gentle, so intuitive, so beautiful. I want to take away the insanity that swirls around us. A gear shifts in my brain and I see everything clearly, for just a moment. She has unlocked everything for me. I realize that if Leo's trying to spare Christine from the dreamworld, he will protect her, even if I cannot. If the other guy kills me, all the problems go away and Christine will not be alone. There is peace to be found, one way or the other.

I smile because this brings me relief.

"It's really going to work out," I say. "And it's all because of you!"

She seems startled. Her forehead creases in the most adorable way.

"You don't think this adds a whole new dimension of bizarre?" she asks. "I mean, there's a secret government agency trying to get you!"

I shrug. "It's not any crazier than visiting a dreamworld. Just about anything seems believable to me."

She doesn't realize the only thing I have to lose is her. I wonder if she's already figured out she was better off before I showed up.

"But doesn't that scare you?"

Sometimes, I forget how selfish I've become. This

isn't life as usual for Christine. She only got sucked into this life a few days ago. Days! I could stand to stop acting like a cavalier ass and consider her feelings.

I can't stand the distance between us anymore, so I pull her into my arms. She wraps hers, lightly, around my waist. The sweet scent of cherry shampoo floats up from her hair. This is the life I want to get used to.

"Nah," I say into her hair. "If your Leo is part of this agency and he's giving you this information, it can't be all bad. You said yourself he isn't creepy."

"He's not, no," she mumbles into my chest. "But everything else is."

My optimism from a moment ago is already disintegrating to ash.

"I think it's going to be okay," I whisper back.

"He said your dad was murdered." Her voice is barely audible and she shivers a little when she says "murdered."

"That's the first thing I've heard about him," I say. It sounds a little cold but it's true.

"I don't like it," she says. Her voice is starting to shake. I can tell she doesn't want it to and that breaks my heart.

"Now it sounds like you're trapped in a seriously dangerous place and no one can help you." Her voice definitely cracks by the end.

"Hey," I say. "You are helping me. You already helped more than anyone else ever has."

She nods into my chest. "I don't want anything to happen to you."

My heart stops momentarily and resets itself. I am overwhelmed that this beautiful girl can care about me at all. I want to give her the world, the universe! But I can't give her those things. I can't even give her myself, as much as I want to. I'm not in control. Won't be until all this dreamworld crap is behind us. But I do have control over some things. I can make damn sure she knows how I feel about her.

29

Christine

"Christine, you're everything to me," he said, the words piercing my heart and humming in my ears.

I had worried that caring wouldn't be enough to save Gabriel, but wrapped firmly in his arms, I saw that I'd been wrong. I'd never be able to protect him from the dreamworld or a secret government agency, but I could anchor him to his own life simply by caring. Maybe we'd both save each other that way.

Hearing him say the words filled me with confidence. I lifted my head from his chest so I could look him in the eye. "I'm glad you got the job at the library."

His eyes were a mix of incredulity, excitement and sorrow. "Me too," he whispered.

As we gazed at each other, our faces separated by mere inches, I was rocked by the sudden feeling that our days together were numbered.

Please don't leave me, I thought.

I'll try not to, is the clear answer that echoed in my brain, even though no one had spoken a word.

30

Christine

The sunlight was bright and comforting. Birds sang and a gentle breeze seemed to follow me down the neighborhood sidewalk. The sounds of children laughing and playing made for a light and happy mood. I stopped walking for a moment and turned my face toward the sun. Michigan girls have to soak up all the sun they can to store up for the long, gray winters.

As I took another step, I realized someone was watching me. Pretending to look for something, I patted my pockets and glanced around. My breath caught when I noticed a young woman in a nearby home staring at me. She looked very pleasant and held a brown-haired baby on her hip. The baby was too busy patting at her face to notice me. The woman smiled, but it didn't reach her bright blue eyes. They were imploring, almost fearful.

Something about her was so compelling that I asked, right out loud, "Do you need help?" Even though I could only bring myself to speak quietly and she was inside her house, I knew she heard me. Without taking her eyes from mine, she held the baby up to the window.

It wiggled and reached toward her face, not looking at me. I couldn't look away as the woman silently exaggerated the words, "Save my baby."

My knees buckled and I crumpled onto the unforgiving concrete. Images created a cyclone in my head until I felt sick. I'd seen that woman and baby before. I'd been on this street. I'd been sucked into the dreamworld again.

I tried to get up, but someone held me down.

"What do you know?" barked an unfamiliar male voice. I hadn't realized my eyes were closed until I opened them. A young blonde man with dark black sunglasses was about a foot from my face, hands clamped on my shoulders, holding me down. Terror kept my lips firmly sealed.

"What do you know?" he yelled again, giving me a little shake for emphasis.

The shake was too much; I couldn't stop myself from vomiting all over his shirt.

"Damn it!" he yelled, jumping back in revulsion. I could only stare as the putrid contents of my stomach dripped down the front of his shirt, heading quickly for his pants.

"Get out of here!" he bellowed at me.

I awoke shaking, with a bitter taste in my mouth. Gabriel was sleeping, curled next to me on the floor. It took a few minutes for reality to click back into place: I'd come over to make the phone call to Leo. But then what happened? It's not like you're just hanging out with someone and you both fall asleep.

I extracted myself as carefully as possible, not wanting to disturb him. I padded to the bathroom to rinse the stinging taste of bile from my mouth, but didn't bother to turn on the light. There was nothing I wanted to see. Swishing the water in my mouth, I thought about the strange man in sunglasses and why he was holding me down until I felt queasy again. I took deep breaths to calm myself and then headed back to Gabriel.

As soon as I saw him, I knew he was in trouble. He was laying flat on his back, jaw and fists clenched.

"No!" I called in vain as I squeezed Gabriel in a bear hug. "Come on, Gabriel. Wake up!"

Nothing happened. Not even the slightest sign he was aware of me.

"There's gotta be something," I panicked to myself. I quickly pressed my lips to his, trying to rouse him with a kiss. I pulled away when I noticed the telltale taste of iron. A crack had appeared on his lower lip and a trickle of blood was beginning to flow from it.

As I watched in horror, the skin on Gabriel's cheek darkened, separated and began to bleed. Understanding hit me like a blow to the stomach; he was under attack and I had to act fast.

I did the only thing I could think of, grabbed my phone and dialed Leo's number. I flung myself over Gabriel's body, instinctively acting as a shield for something I couldn't protect against.

Leo's phone rang and rang. I was beginning to think I'd dialed the wrong number before he finally answered.

"Leo, I can't wake him up! Someone is hurting him and I can't wake him up! You have to help me!"

That was all it took for Leo to snap into action. "Whoa! What do you mean someone is hurting him?"

"I'm right next to him and cuts and bruises are appearing all over his face, I can't just sit here—" I couldn't finish the sentence.

"Shit! Someone must have found him, but they shouldn't be attacking him."

I felt Gabriel's body trembling, as if reacting to a volley of invisible blows. "Think faster! It's getting worse!"

Leo exhaled loudly. "Of all the times for this to happen. I'm not on duty right now!"

"Just tell me what to do!"

"You can't do anything," he said, aggravation heavy in his voice. "If you can't wake him up, it's because someone locked him in. Someone has to override the signal, but I'm not on duty. I'll have to call my superior but then she'll know about both of you. Damn! I didn't want this to happen to you."

A slash tore through the shoulder of Gabriel's shirt and blood began seeping through.

"Forget about me!" I screamed. "They're going to kill him!"

I pressed my hands to his shoulder in an effort to stop the bleeding. The warmth of the blood against my skin sickened me but I had to feel like I was doing something.

"Okay, I need your location so they can do a

manual trace of the frequency."

"What?"

"Gimme your address!"

"I'm at Gabriel's. I don't know the address!"

"Look for mail," Leo said.

Reluctant to let up on Gabriel's shoulder, my eyes darted around the room desperate to spot a piece of junk mail.

The trashcan in the kitchen seemed to be my best hope. I raced to the trash and had never been so relieved to find a credit card application. I recited the address to Leo and he clicked over to call his superior. I only hoped whatever they needed to do was a fast process.

Time seemed to move in slow motion, yet the wounds over Gabriel's body appeared quickly. His knuckles reddened and cracked as I imagined he fought back.

"Hang on, Gabriel," I said, for my own benefit. "We're going to get you out of this."

Gabriel drew in a long ragged breath and his eyes fluttered open. His strong face was bruised and blood-ied, but as his eyes found mine, I thought he'd never looked more beautiful.

"Thank God!" Tears streamed down my face. I rested my cheek on his chest and sobbed into his warm body. Slowly, with some wincing, he moved his arm over my back and snaked his fingers into my hair.

"That was rough," he whispered.

I hugged him as gently as I could. "What hurts worst? Should we go to a doctor?"

Before he could formulate an answer, I noticed the phone, which had fallen near Gabriel's knee, making a strange noise.

I picked it up and realized Leo was yelling to get my attention. "IS HE OKAY?" Leo shouted in my ear.

"Yes, sorry. He's awake." I looked down at him, lying tensely. "He needs to get fixed up, but he's awake. I gotta go take care of him. *Thank you*, Leo."

"Hang on, Christine. We have to talk," Leo said.

"But the blood—" I said, biting my lip.

Gabriel wiggled his fingers at me in an "it can wait a minute" gesture.

"Okay," I conceded. "What is it?"

"I'm going to need a lot of information from you about what happened today. At this point, I've been granted permission to take the report. I've also been given the official order to protect you."

"Me? What about Gabriel?"

"Don't worry, he's got a whole team looking after him now."

That bit of news served as a relief as much as a stressor. A whole team? What kind of danger were we up against?

"I want you to call me the second anything unusual happens to you, in the dreamworld or otherwise."

"How do I call you in the dreamworld?" I asked.

"I'm linked to your frequency now," he answered. "I'll be monitoring all your dream activity, but you'll probably be able to sense danger quicker than I can see from outside the dream. Just call my name, I'll be right there. There's no such thing as a false alarm."

I swallowed the lump that had suddenly lodged in my throat.

"This is all really weird," I said.

Gabriel gingerly reached for my hand and attempted a reassuring squeeze. The momentary grimace that appeared on his face as a result had the opposite effect.

"I know," Leo said gently. "I'm sorry you got dragged into this, but our best agents are on it now. I promise to make this as easy for you as I can."

"Thank you," I said, grateful for the sentiment, even though we both knew there could be nothing easy about this situation.

"Okay then. Take care of yourselves and try to relax. Remember, I'm here if you need anything."

I hung up the phone and turned back to Gabriel. His eyes were closed.

"Don't go to sleep!" I said louder than I'd intended.

Gabriel tried to smile, but the action re-split his lip and the blood started flowing fresh.

"Don't move!" I ordered. "I gotta get some things to clean you up, I'll be right back."

I darted to the kitchen to get some towels and ice.

"There's a first aid kit in the bathroom medicine cabinet," he called after me.

I changed course and headed for the bathroom. I flung open the door to the cabinet. The only thing in it was a few prescription bottles and the first aid kit.

After gathering supplies, I knelt next to Gabriel

and got to work tending his wounds. He tried hard not to flinch, but I could tell he was hurt pretty bad.

"Who did this to you?" I asked, dabbing at his raw cheek with a cold washcloth.

"Some asshole blond guy."

"Did you recognize him?"

Gabriel looked away. On instinct, I decided he'd been hiding something.

"What did he look like?" I continued to press.

"He was wearing sunglasses, so I couldn't really see what he looked like."

I stopped bandaging up Gabriel's hand and looked him in the eye. In my haste to protect him, I had forgotten about my own encounter.

"What happened to you?" Understanding stole into his gaze without me saying a word.

"I saw him too. He held me down and asked what I knew."

Despite the pain, Gabriel pushed himself up and hugged me as tight as he could. "I'm so sorry."

"Stop it. It isn't your fault. Besides, I threw up on him and then I was back here with you."

"You threw up on him?"

"Yeah, well, I was feeling sorta sick before he got to me. But that's not very important. Did he say anything to you?"

"Christine, this is important. That guy wasn't playing around and it makes me sick to think he was messing with you. If something happened to you, I would never forgive myself."

"Leo said we were both under protection now."

Gabriel looked tense all over again. "I should be able to protect you myself."

I sat up straight. "There shouldn't be anything for you to protect me from. This isn't a normal situation. You can't blame yourself."

"I do. You wouldn't be in this nightmare if it wasn't for me."

"Don't say that," I said putting my hand on his arm. He gently removed my hand and stood up.

"What are you doing?" I asked.

"I gotta go," he answered, his eyes darting around the room like he expected an enemy to pop out at any second.

"Where?" I demanded. I didn't like his tone or the darkness in his eyes.

"I just need to think." He started pacing and laced his fingers into his hair.

"Can't you think here?" I asked. "Shouldn't we stay together?" I didn't want to sound needy, but if that could break though the crisis he was having, so be it.

"Yes, probably," he said. There was no disguising the frustration in his voice, but I didn't know what or whom it was directed at.

He headed into the bathroom and I heard the distinctive click of the medicine cabinet door. The sound reminded me of the pill bottles, which made me shiver.

He emerged a few seconds later and, this time, headed for the door.

"What are you doing?" I asked, jumping up from

the bed, but not knowing what to do once I was on my feet.

"I'm so sorry," he replied in a thick voice, not even turning back to look at me. "I'll be back," and he walked out the door.

31

Gabriel

I know I'm being a complete asshole, but I can't control it. I have to leave Christine right now before she sees any more. Maybe she'll forgive me later, but right now, I have to go. I have to get away from here. I have to get out of my head.

I want to scream or smash the windows out of these cars, but I still have enough sense left to know that would get me locked up.

I break into a run, wishing as I've done a million times before that I could run away from myself. I run right out of the parking lot. It would be too dangerous to drive and the running actually makes me feel slightly better. At least I feel like I'm doing something. Yet, it doesn't dull the buzzing sensation that is slowly over-taking my body.

The scenery rushing past me makes me feel like I'm in a chase scene from a movie. The only thing chasing me now is the memory of how close that guy came to killing me, just minutes ago. Minutes ago! I want to scream as I realize my face is starting to feel warm and wet. Bleeding again. Bleeding and running down the street. I'll be lucky if I'm not arrested for suspicious behavior.

The irony strikes me. The lucky thing about the real world is everybody minds their own business. As long as I've waited for someone to care, I'm actually grateful now that nobody will. Bloody guy tearing down the sidewalk? Oh well. Best not to get involved.

The only person who does care; I left her standing in my apartment. Alone and scared.

I can't even hate myself properly because this whole thing is taking over my mind.

Just run. Run!

I focus on my feet as they make contact with the pavement. Their thump, thump is real. Grounding. So is the rush of my breath. Thump, thump, exhale. Thump, thump, inhale. Thump, thump, exhale.

The pill slowly begins to take hold. The only thing that can save me when I get like this. But I don't want Christine to see me in either state. Manic or drugged-up. And for that stupid reason, alone, I'm running; running away from the only person I want to stay with more than anything.

32

Christine

I was lost.

I knew things I didn't want to know. Gabriel had just been attacked in a different plane of reality. And I was sitting alone in his apartment, having watched him flee, possibly forever.

One thing was certain: this wasn't right.

Shock was beginning to give way to resolve. Why was I sitting around? Gabriel was hurt and scared. I couldn't let him run from me.

I jumped up and bolted out the door, letting my body guide me. It wasn't long before I realized I was heading toward the park. I came around the corner of the parking lot and spotted him ahead. He was definitely going for the park, too. Looked like he was starting to slow down a little, so I kicked it into high gear.

"Hey!" I yelled, sounding more authoritative than I felt. "Gabriel, don't you dare leave me!"

He'd just reached an intersection he couldn't cross, so he turned around and stopped. I was already gulping for breath, completely unused to so much exertion, but I couldn't let him get away. I kept running until I reached him.

"Caught ya," I panted. "Let's not play this game again."

"Please go," he said in a quiet voice. "I'm not myself right now."

"I don't care," I said. "We're in this together. You can't just run away."

"I know," he said, his voice flat. "But I didn't want you to see what I'm like on this stuff."

"What stuff?" I asked. My exhaustion giving way to wariness.

"One pill to make me sleepy. One to make me calm," he answered.

Daria would have a field day with this.

"Gabriel," I said placing my hand on his arm. "What did you take?"

"It makes the crazy go away," he said.

"Are you okay?" I asked, beginning to wonder if I needed to call an ambulance. "You're kinda scaring me."

"I didn't want you to see," he said, turning his face away. "I usually just sleep it off. I'm me again when I wake up. Don't worry."

I needed to proceed with caution, but I had to know. "Gabriel, are you supposed to be taking that stuff?"

His eyes shot back to mine in alarm.

"Yes!" he exclaimed. "I have anxiety problems thanks to this whole mess. Sometimes it gets so bad I can't function. My doctor prescribed them for me. They're powerful, but they're mine."

I looked away, embarrassed that I'd essentially accused of him of being a druggie.

"It's okay," he said, taking my hands in his. "Sometimes it just hits me so fast I start freaking out and I can't think. I should have explained it to you before, but I didn't want to give you another reason to think I'm a psycho."

I stared at his broken face, the bloodstains on his shirt, and knew exactly what to do. Gentle as possible, I pressed my lips to his. I didn't flinch away from the copper taste of his blood. All I wanted was to be as close to him as possible.

I pulled away and noticed he was trembling. Afraid I'd hurt one of his new injuries, I gasped. "Are you all right?"

His eyes bored into mine. "Christine, I love you," he whispered. The words charged the air around me like an electrical storm.

"Come on," I said gently. "Let's get you back to the apartment." I started walking back but he stopped me.

"I mean it," he said. "It isn't the pills talking."

"I know," I answered. "I think I love you too."

He smiled, causing blood to spill down his chin.

"You're a mess, you know that?" I giggled.

He smeared the blood away with the back of his hand. "You make me feel invincible," he said.

For just a moment, I pretended we really were.

33

Christine

Gabriel had been dozing, under my watchful eye, since I'd brought him back to his apartment. I didn't like that he was sleeping, and therefore more vulnerable to the dreamworld, but it was the best medicine for him.

As he slept, I studied his face for any sign of distress. Every twitch had me clutching my phone, ready to call Leo, until I saw him relax again.

When my phone unexpectedly rang, I answered on the first ring, half from surprise and half to keep it from waking Gabriel.

"Hello," I whispered as I slid off Gabriel's bed.

"Are you ready to hear the best news of your life?" Tiffany exclaimed.

She didn't know how ready I was for some good news.

"Sounds great but this isn't—"

"Marcel is taking me to France!" If her exclamation had been any more high-pitched, it would have burst my eardrum.

"Wait, he's what?" It was like my brain had to

physically shift gears to follow the conversation.

The sound of Tiffany's laughter helped bring me back to the land of normalcy.

"Marcel's going home for a visit before the summer's over and he asked me to go with him!"

"Are you kidding me?" Excitement crept over me, despite the reality waiting for me in the other room. "What did your parents say?"

"They don't know yet," Tiffany confessed. "But there's no way they can say no. This is a once in a lifetime chance!"

"Wow, Tiff! I don't even know what to say."

Tiffany squealed and I held the phone away from my ear until she came back to a reasonable decibel.

"I can't believe this is really happening! I'm going to need an all-new wardrobe for France. So, I'm actually calling to see if you want to go shopping with me later on."

"Yeah, of course." I answered. "Just stop by tonight when you're ready. I should be at Daria's by then."

"Oh, really?" Tiffany's voice held a conspiratorial tone. "And where are you right now, I wonder."

"Gabriel's not feeling well," I said, which wasn't a lie at all. "I'm taking care of him."

"Does Daria know?" she asked.

"Sort of."

"See? She's lightening up already." I could hear the grin in her voice. "Anyway, I'll let you get back to your patient. Just had to make sure you were the first to know."

I know she didn't say it to be mean but it made me feel guilty anyway. There was so much I couldn't tell her, things she could never know, but I was still number one on her list. It meant more than ever before.

"Thanks, Tiff," I said, a wave of emotion coming over me.

"No problem," she continued. "See ya later!"

"Yeah, that'll be great," I said.

When I opened the bathroom door to leave, Gabriel was on his way in. He walked stiffly, gingerly picking out each step to minimize the pain.

"Oh!" he startled when he noticed me. "I thought you must have left."

"No," I said. "I was keeping an eye on you to make sure nothing bad happened but Tiffany called and I came in here so I wouldn't disturb you." I assessed his condition with a heavy heart. "Are you sure you don't want me to take you to the doctor? You look so uncomfortable."

"I'll be fine." He tried to assure me by pulling me close.

I found a tiny spot along his jaw that wasn't bruised or cut and I softly placed my lips to it.

"I'm feeling better already," he said.

He was so brave. I didn't know how he managed it.

My phone chimed to let me know a new text had come in. I glanced down at it.

"You can check it," he said. "I've got some business to attend to." He shuffled his way into the bathroom and shut the door.

The text was from my mom. Another photo of carpet samples for my new room. It was a good thing she couldn't see my lack of enthusiasm. "Looks great!" I texted back, hoping to be rid of the whole pointless conversation.

When Gabriel returned, I told him about Tiffany's phone call. Now that I was looking at his face, leaving him for a shopping trip didn't seem like such a great idea.

"Don't worry about me," he said. "You should go have fun with your friend."

I chewed my bottom lip.

"Hey, it's fine," he said. "I've got a whole team to protect me now, right? Go."

I gave him a gentle peck on the lips. "Okay, just be careful anyway. I'll call as soon as I'm back."

"I'll be right here waiting."

I turned to go, knowing I'd never forgive myself if something happened to him and hoping I wouldn't be put to the test.

34

Christine

I sat on the squeaky old swing slowly dragging my toes in the dirt. It was the lazy kind of summer day that seems like it'll never end but is all too quickly gone. The heat was uncomfortable but bearable as long as I didn't move much. My skin was covered in a thin sheen of stickiness. Someone had been smart enough to put the swing next to an enormous oak tree, so I wasn't in the direct sunlight. The tree was impressively wide and I wondered how many generations of people had passed beneath its branches.

My thoughts were interrupted by a cough close behind me. I leapt off the swing and whirled around to find a guy standing about four feet behind me.

"Ever think of saying 'hello' before you creep up on someone?" I asked with a bitterness that surprised me.

He didn't seem to mind. His dark sunglasses made it impossible to tell where he was looking. Without the cues of eye contact, I didn't know where to look, so my eyes darted from his blonde hair, short frame and sinewy build. I don't know why it occurred to me, but he looked very fast.

He put a lit cigarette to his lips, I hadn't noticed that before, and took a long drag before he said anything. "Don't be so touchy."

His voice jarred my brain. This was the same guy who had held me down and attacked Gabriel. Instead of filling me with fear, the realization spurred rage.

"Who are you?" I asked with uncharacteristic force.

He shrugged. "Doesn't matter."

"Funny. It matters to me. If you're not going to tell me who you are and what you're doing here—"

"Down girl. Take it easy. Do you give your boyfriend this much trouble?" He smirked.

"Get out of my dream," I snarled in a voice so laced with venom it didn't sound like my own.

He dropped his cigarette and squashed it into the ground with his shoe.

"Well, well, well. It appears we have a lot to talk about," he said, taking a step toward me.

"There is nothing to talk about," I hissed. "Unless you tell me who you are."

He opened his arms in a gesture I could only assume meant he wasn't threatening me. I didn't buy it. He took another step closer.

"I'm not asking you again," I said, the blood rushing in my ears from the furious pumping of my heart.

He smiled. "What's a name? Nothing but a word. But since you are so hung up on this, I'll tell you. I'm Brett. Now will you repay the favor or should we just get on with things?"

"There's nothing to get on with," I said.

"On the contrary," said Brett, if I could believe he'd given a real name. "There's quite a bit for us to take care of. The only thing lacking is time, so how about we quit wasting it?"

The mocking tone in his voice made me so angry I wanted to attack him. Just as I contemplated throwing my first punch ever, I heard a voice from behind me.

"Get away from her!" Gabriel shouted.

I turned to see him running toward us. His voice sounded like he was right behind me, but he was several yards away. Still, seeing him released a little of the vice grip tension held on my stomach.

Time seemed to have slowed down as he made his way toward me. I didn't want to stand there like a princess waiting to be rescued, so I decided to run to him. The moment the thought entered my head, Brett grabbed me from behind and wrapped me in a bear hug that practically squeezed all the air from my lungs.

"Come any closer and it's over for her!" Brett yelled.

Gabriel froze mid-stride and seemed to hover in the air for a minute before his feet settled on the ground like normal.

"What do you want from me?" Gabriel asked. He didn't mask the anguish in his voice and it broke my heart.

"Haven't you guessed by now?" Brett snarled. "I want you gone."

"I don't even know you," Gabriel said in a steely voice I didn't recognize.

"Yes, that's true," agreed Brett, in a tone not much different than Gabriel's. "But I know you very well. I know all about you and, I'm sorry to say, we are not compatible."

"Then why don't you leave me alone?" Gabriel said in a low voice.

"That isn't an option," Brett said.

"This is bullshit and we're going to end it now," Gabriel snarled, slowly inching forward.

Instantly, a knife glinted at my neck. "I already warned you about coming any closer. Don't care about your little girlfriend anymore?"

Gabriel stopped. "Why don't you be a man and leave her out of it? If it's me you want, come get me."

Brett's rage was as palpable as the sharp blade at my throat. He shoved me aside, knocking me to the ground, and ran toward Gabriel.

Gabriel let loose a war cry and launched himself at Brett in a magnificent, supernatural leap. As he reached the apex of his arc, Brett roared and held up his hand. Instantly, Gabriel's body ceased to exist. In its place were countless dazzling stars. They twinkled and swirled furiously in only the space Gabriel's leaping body had just occupied. In slow motion, Star Gabriel continued the trajectory of his course and when he should have landed at Brett's feet, he crashed into a shower of sparks that hissed along the ground until, one by one, they went dark.

35

Gabriel

I am soaring through the air in an unnatural way. People only move like this in movies, suspended in air through the aid of special effects, but this is real. My desire to get this asshole away from Christine allows me to do the impossible. For once in my life, I will triumph.

I can see the seconds until we collide. They streak before me like shooting stars. Getting brighter, brighter. Blinding me…

Now, I am trapped in a cold, heavy substance that feels like Jell-O. I can't move. It's difficult to breathe, but my vision is clearer than ever and what I see crushes my chest like a lead weight.

Christine is screaming on the ground. Her eyes probe mine, wild with fear, but she doesn't seem to see me. I want to explode. But first, I want to smash that laughing bastard to pieces. Yet I can only stare and ache with my desire that he doesn't hurt her.

He finally has his fill of laughter and covers his ears, turning to her as he does.

"Shut up!" he bellows.

She does, but her mouth doesn't close and she doesn't take her eyes from me. They gaze right through me, radiating a pain she's kept carefully hidden since this all began.

I have done this to her.

I force myself to keep looking into her eyes because it makes me hurt so badly. I deserve it.

The mad man sighs and a satisfied smirk settles on his face.

"Well, now that I've annihilated him, what are we going to do about you? Can't have you showing up here anymore." He crosses his arms and looks at Christine. She looks so broken, on the ground like that.

Before she can answer, a man with a blonde ponytail appears beside her. He is already crouching, placing a hand gently on her shoulder. His touch causes her to turn toward him. There is no mistaking the relief flooding her eyes when she sees him. It pierces my heart like a rusty blade.

"Don't worry, Christine," he says and his voice sounds like it's right next to my ear. "It's not what it seems."

She nods slightly and throws her arms around this guy. He doesn't miss a beat wrapping her in his own. He turns his head to the side so I can see his profile now. His nose is cut at a severe angle that almost reminds me of a beak.

So this is Leo.

My view is blocked as two familiar people also appear on either side of the mad man. It's the giant dude and the Anime chick who were looking for me on the beach.

The girl has a little device in her hand and she uses it to zap Mad Man in the head. He crumples to the ground without any resistance and the big guy grabs a handful of Mad Man's shirt and picks him up like nothing.

I was right about those two.

Now I get a new companion. A girl in a tight black tank top and army green cargo pants appears in front of me and my Jell-O prison disappears. Off balance, I fall to the ground.

She reaches out to help me up, but I shake my head. I'd rather dissolve into the dirt than be helped by her when I couldn't do a thing to help Christine.

A smile spreads across her lips. There's no masking the happiness in her brown eyes as she looks at me and says, "Welcome home, Gabriel Chase."

36

Christine

I opened my eyes and Daria's living room came into focus. My chest ached with the rapid beating of my heart.

A tentative knock came at the door. Disoriented, I rubbed my forehead and stumbled from the couch to the door, with a vague idea that it must be Gabriel.

Peeking through the peephole, I gasped when I saw Leo's face.

"Christine, please let me in," he said quietly. My gasp must have given me away.

Pulling open the door, thoughts formed and crumbled in my brain before I could acknowledge them. Seeing Leo outside of the dreamworld jarred me in a way I wouldn't have expected. I knew he was real, but it still felt like he was just some guy I dreamed about. Standing in the doorway, I couldn't pretend things weren't what they seemed. Now, I had to admit, things were pretty terrifying.

Being with Leo, in reality, seemed different somehow. I could see him clearly for a change, without the perfect darkness of a Wyoming night to obscure him.

He wore a powder-blue t-shirt, which emphasized the dramatic blue of his eyes. I met his gaze, feeling suddenly shy, but his expression relaxed me. A tendril of his blonde hair had come loose from his ponytail and fell against his cheek. I sucked in a breath of air, fighting the sudden urge to smooth away the stray hair for him.

"May I come in?" he asked.

"Of course," I answered, moving aside.

He slipped past, careful not to brush against me.

"Do you want to sit down?" I asked, gesturing to the couch.

"Yeah, thanks," he said, making his way toward it.

I sat on the opposite end, our last dreamworld encounter slowly put itself together in my mind.

"I should explain why I'm here," he said, folding his hands between his knees.

I nodded.

"First, I wanted to guarantee your safety. As soon as we got Gabriel stabilized from his attack, I went to the airport and bought a ticket for the first flight to Detroit. Now, you have to understand, this isn't how I do things. No agent shows up on your doorstep, really, but you are a very special case." He shook his head. "Special person. I want to make sure you're given all your options, and we can't be monitored here in the real world. Do you understand?"

He looked at me, nervous excitement radiating through the air. What I could understand was that he wasn't supposed to be sitting in the living room with me, but he'd come anyway.

"I don't understand anything," I said.

A smirk flickered across his lips and he looked away. "Of course you don't. You're so good at all this, it's easy to imagine you've gone through all the training."

I nodded even though I still didn't get what he meant.

He exhaled slowly. "Where should I start?" he asked, not looking at me.

"Well," I offered. "It would be nice to know what happened to Gabriel."

His eyebrows shot up. "Yes!" he exclaimed. "Sorry, I should have said that right away. He's in the protection of our top agent. They're probably having a similar conversation right now."

A knot in my stomach, that I hadn't been conscious of, relaxed.

"Okay," I said, rubbing my head. "Would you mind telling me what just happened in the dreamworld? I'm having trouble remembering."

Leo's jaw tightened.

"I wondered about that. The traitor used a few mind applications on you."

"What?" I didn't like the sound of that.

Leo held his hands up. "It doesn't cause any permanent damage. It just allows agents to manipulate how you perceive the dreamscape. For instance, judging from your reaction, you didn't see that Gabriel was there, unharmed, the whole time."

I squinted, as if I could peer back through my memory. I couldn't remember what I'd seen, but I did know I'd felt scared and alone.

When I didn't respond, he gestured toward me. "That would be the memory lock. It's standard procedure, actually. It prevents you from forming solid memories while in the dream state. It also occurs naturally. That's why people don't remember most of their dreams."

"You can do that to people?"

"Yes. It's necessary in this line of work. But it isn't taken lightly."

"Why do you…" I couldn't finish the question, not entirely sure I wanted to know.

Leo frowned slightly. "That's something I can't tell you, even though I've given away so much already."

I nodded. That was something I could understand.

"Well, what happens now?" I asked.

Leo sat up straight and turned to me.

"Well, there are a number of possibilities."

"Any of them good?"

He cocked his head as he considered the question, but didn't break eye contact with me.

"It depends on what you want," he said, at last.

That was a loaded statement. What did I want? It was hard to be sure anymore.

Luckily, he didn't wait for an answer.

"My superior is intrigued by you. You seem to have crossed into the dreamworld without being summoned. That doesn't usually happen. In fact, it's only been documented twice in our history; by Gabriel and his father, Agent Richard Chase."

I leaned back against the couch as the hairs on the back of my neck stood at attention.

"Are you okay?" Leo asked as he covered the distance between us on the couch but didn't touch me.

"This is crazy," I said. "What can any of it mean?"

"Maybe we should talk about something else for awhile. This is a lot to take in at once."

"There's no way I can think about anything else," I said.

"Are you excited about senior year?" he asked.

"What?"

"When we first met, you said you'd just finished your junior year. Are you excited?"

"Not exactly," I confessed. "But you remember that?"

Leo looked away and scooted back to his original spot at the other end of the couch.

"Yeah, that sort of thing interests me."

"You work for a secret government agency and you think my school-excitement level is interesting?"

His cheeks reddened, just the slightest bit.

"Let's just say I sometimes wonder how things could have been."

"What things?" I asked.

He sighed heavily and stared at the ceiling a minute before he answered.

"Life. I forget what it's like to be normal, sometimes."

"Tell me about it," I said, sinking back into the couch.

His lips curved upward but it wasn't really a smile, more of an agreement.

"How did you get into all this, anyway?" I asked. "Did you actually have a choice?"

"I'm not really supposed to talk about that with non-recruits. However," he lowered his voice. "That is one of your options."

"What?"

"Since you've already entered the dreamworld, un-summoned and in a fully-aware state, you can be recruited for dream work. If you want."

He said each word carefully and quietly, but his eyes burned with an incongruous intensity. I could tell he had a strong opinion on what I should think of this option, but I couldn't tell if he was for or against.

"What does that mean, exactly?" I asked just as carefully.

"It means you can pursue dream work, at training camp, like Gabriel will. But you need to understand it's a long, fairly solitary process. It's a mentorship program. You wouldn't be permitted to interact with the other recruits until your training was complete."

"And how many recruits are there?"

"Technically, it would just be you and Gabriel. We aren't a big agency and we only seek out those with natural abilities."

"First," I said, finally feeling like I could get a grasp on all this. "Gabriel hates the dreamworld. I'm not sure he's going to sign up for any training. And second, how long does this training take?"

"Eighteen months to three years, depending on natural aptitude, but eighteen months minimum is required."

"How long did it take you?"

"Twenty-six months."

"And you didn't see anybody for all that time? What about your family?"

He stiffened.

"Family wasn't an issue. I don't have any. I worked with my mentor. You have to understand, it's a completely life-consuming process. You have to immerse yourself to master it. It's very difficult, rigorous work."

I tried to imagine a complete 180 from my current job working with the public and my friends. How could anyone spend up to three years in a secret training camp with only their mentor to see everyday? What if you didn't get along with them? What if I was paired with someone like Brett? I swallowed down a rising wave of fear. We needed to talk about something else.

"And what are my other options?"

"If you don't want to recruit, we can do a more powerful memory lock on you that will make you forget everything associated with the dreamworld. It would be like waking up from a strange dream you can't quite remember."

Our conversation could have been lifted from the script of a sci-fi movie. The thought made me feel a little dizzy.

"So basically, I have one option. Join or lose my memories."

Leo shuffled his feet.

That was enough of a confirmation.

"What about you and Gabriel?" I asked.

"What about us?"

"Would I still know you? If I didn't join."

He shook his head.

"You might remember Gabriel because you knew him outside of the dreamworld first, but you'd have no recollection of me."

The heaviness in my chest was surprisingly intense. I'd grown to rely on Leo as a voice of reason amidst a reality spiraling out of control. He was my only confidante. How could I just let him go?

"You don't need to decide anything right now," he said gently.

"What do you want me to do?" I asked.

"It isn't up to me," he answered quickly.

I shrugged. "That isn't the issue. You wouldn't have come here if you didn't care. I want to know what you really think."

He shook his head. "I don't want to influence your decision."

"What if I want you to?"

His eyebrows shot up in surprise but he turned away.

"No," he said. "At least, not yet. You need some time to think about it first."

I groaned. "Do you have to be so frustrating?"

He chuckled. "It's part of the job."

37

Gabriel

I look into the eyes of this girl who's welcoming me home. There is joy in them. There's excitement. She must be horribly mistaken.

I shake my head. "Sorry," I say. "This isn't my home."

She actually laughs. And it's a big laugh. It makes the springy black curls of her hair bounce playfully. They're pulled back from her forehead by a wide head-band but it only redirects them into a curly explosion around her head. I can't help myself – I want to touch those wild curls. Everything about this girl seems so charged with life, I wonder if those spirals would shock me.

She holds out her hand again, her lips peeled into a wide smile. "I'm Agent Zemma Garr," she says.

This time, I take her hand. She doesn't shock me but she does grip my hand firmly. Not so hard that it hurts, but enough that I know this woman isn't to be messed with.

"I'm Gabriel Gray," I say. "Not Chase."

She nods. "I'm sorry," she says, still gripping my

hand. "Your father was Agent Richard Chase. We didn't know what happened to you, but we assumed you'd kept your name."

I shake my head, withdrawing my hand from hers and pushing back my hair. "Uh, no. I was adopted by the Gray family."

"Well, that explains some things," she says.

I don't know what needs to be explained about me, but there are definitely things I need to know. Now.

"Where is Christine?" I ask.

A flicker of confusion passes over Zemma's face before she realizes what I mean.

"Oh, your girl? Agent Bonaventure's got her."

"Leo?"

"Yes, have you met?"

"No, but Christine has seen him before." I try not to think about the way she looked at him.

"He's a good guy. She'll be well taken care of."

That's what I'm afraid of.

"Why couldn't I move?" I ask, forcing the image of Christine clinging to Leo from my mind.

"Traitorous Agent Lawrence deployed a mind trap on you." Her nose wrinkles like she smells something bad. "He had some nerve messing with the son of Agent Chase, but we'll take care of him. In the meantime, once we get you into training, you won't be susceptible to maneuvers like that anymore."

"Whoa, whoa, whoa!" I exclaim. "What do you mean, get me into training?"

Her deep, brown eyes transform to pools of

innocence before the fire comes back.

"Your father was the greatest agent who ever lived. His staggering natural aptitude has been passed on to, if not exceeded by, you."

She cocks her head and places her slender hands on her hips. "Do you believe in destiny?"

I shrug. "I don't know what I believe anymore."

"Then believe me, Gabriel Gray. You were born for this. There's nowhere you belong more than here."

She says the words with authority, as if she's investing me with an ancient charge. Everything about her exudes power, the set of her jaw, the square of her shoulders, the hard angles of her elbows. Her eyes are strong and serious now. The joy of finding me has been replaced by the strength of her conviction, the conviction that I am great. In her eyes is more confidence in me than I've ever had in myself.

She stands before me, firmly planted on the ground. Firmly planted in her assurance. There is nothing else I can do.

I believe her.

38

Christine

I was surprised to hear another knock at my door. Leo had suggested we watch TV for a while, since I had a lot to think about and I didn't want him to leave. That's what we were doing when I opened the door, expecting to see Gabriel on the other side. Who I never expected to see was Tiffany.

"Why didn't you answer your phone?" she asked as she punched me in the arm and pushed her way through the door. She stopped short when she caught sight of Leo, who immediately stood up to greet her.

"Whoa, am I interrupting?" Tiffany asked, her eyes practically popping out of her head.

"No," Leo and I said at the same time.

"We're only watching TV," I said, at the same time Leo said, "I was just about to go."

"Don't leave because of me," Tiffany said.

"Leo," I said, "This is my best friend, Tiffany. Tiffany, this is Leo."

Leo extended his hand to Tiffany who quickly stepped in to shake it.

"So," said Tiffany, shooting me a meaningful look.

"How did you two meet?"

"I'm a friend of Gabriel's," Leo said without a second of hesitation.

Tiffany narrowed her eyes, trying to drill the truth out of me subliminally.

"Is he lurking around here somewhere too?" Tiffany asked.

"No," I said carefully. "Leo's just chilling out with me since Gabriel's not feeling well."

Tiffany's eyes said, "You're such a liar" but her lips curved into a pleasant smile.

"Well, it's very nice to meet you, Leo," she said turning her gaze from me. "I hope you'll excuse me while I talk to my friend for a minute."

Leo nodded. "I'll take a walk," he said.

I started to protest but he shut me down. "I won't go far."

As soon as the door closed behind him, Tiffany turned on me. "What the heck is that all about?"

"Nothing," I said, too tired to come up with more lies.

"Yeah, right. Looked like a pretty cozy nothing to me."

"Please," I pleaded.

Tiffany fixed me in an appraising stare. "You're so weird these days. I almost feel like I don't know you anymore."

I sunk back into the couch and put my head in my hands. "Don't turn into Daria on me."

"Does she know about this guy?" She gestured

toward the door like Leo was still standing there.

"No, I just met him today. Could we talk about something else? Really, there's no story here."

"Yeah, sure. Is he coming too?" Tiffany asked.

"Coming where?" I was completely confused.

"Did you seriously forget already?" Tiffany crossed her arms and stared me down.

She didn't know a traitorous government secret agent had been tampering with my memory.

"No," I said. "I didn't forget anything."

Tiffany shook her head. "You're so full of it! Shopping for France. Does that ring any bells?"

I dropped my hands to my sides in defeat. She'd caught me being a crappy friend but there was no way I could go shopping now.

"Sorry," I said. "I'm feeling a little off today myself."

"Aww," she brightened. "You're already sharing sicknesses. So cute!"

"Any possibility we can postpone the shopping trip?" I asked.

Tiffany screwed up her mouth and tapped her chin as she pondered the question. "Well," she considered. "Daria should be off work soon. Maybe I'll pick her up. She has better fashion sense than you, anyway."

At least she was taking it with humor.

"Ok, I'll let you flake out on me this time, but only because you have that secret love life thing going on. However," she paused and pointed at me, "If you don't spill the beans the second that guy leaves tonight I will, absolutely, kill you."

"Yes, yes," I said. "I promise."

She stared at me a moment longer to make sure I understood the seriousness of the situation.

"I will!" I exclaimed.

"Okay then. I really am going to get Daria, you know. So, she might be late getting back tonight. Au revoir!" she called over her shoulder as she showed herself out.

I leaned back in the couch, exhausted by my life. But, before I could begin to wonder where Leo had gone, I heard a soft knock at the door. I jumped up and let him back in.

"Sorry about that," I said. "I forgot I was supposed to go shopping with her."

He looked stricken. "I hope I didn't mess up your girl time."

"Ha!" I laughed. "I'm not very good at girl time anymore. Got bigger things on my mind these days."

He looked somber. "I wish I could be more of a help."

I turned to stare at Leo, the feelings solidifying even before the words could form in my mind.

"What's wrong?" he asked, leaning closer to me.

"You understand," I said.

At that moment, he didn't look like he understood anything. I would have laughed if realization hadn't held such a strong grip on me.

"You understand everything," I continued. "You understand why Gabriel acts so impulsively. You understand the dreamworld and the real world. You understand…" suddenly feeling self-conscious, I could scarcely say the next word, "…me."

Leo looked very serious.

"Maybe I should go," he said. "I'm influencing you just by being here."

"No," I said, louder than I'd meant to. "Please stay with me."

He slowly sank onto the couch and I exhaled the breath I'd been holding.

He took the liberty of turning the TV back on and I found myself stealthily staring at him instead of the screen, trying to imagine going back to a life without him and Gabriel in it.

39

Gabriel

"We should get started right away," Zemma says, her urgency infectious. "Pack what you can fit in a duffle bag and we'll get you set up at training camp."

"What's the rush?" I ask.

"Make up for lost time!" She says it like it's the most obvious thing in the world. "With ability like yours, you'll be head of this agency in no time."

Her words are terrifying and exhilarating. Me? The head of something important? I wonder if she has me confused with some other guy. Maybe I'm not the Gabriel they're looking for.

"You keep talking about natural ability, but how do you know I have any?"

She laughs again.

"Agent Gray, we've been looking for you a long time. We've been tracking frequency bursts, which have been getting larger over time, but you're still elusive. Given the strength of your frequency and your ability to remain undetected, you're going to be one kick-ass agent. Once I get you trained, of course."

She gives me a sly grin.

"You're going to train me?" I ask even though that's what she just said.

"Yes, sir. I'm the best they've got, until you're finished. We're going to make a great team. I can see that already."

"But what about Christine?" Zemma might be anxious to get on with training, but I need to see Christine.

"Leo's with her. She's fine."

"I got that, but when can I see her?"

"Oh." Zemma stops, as if she hadn't anticipated this possibility. "No visits once training begins."

"What?"

"It's an intense regimen. A full life training. You pretty much say goodbye to the outside world and become a full-time agent."

This is starting to go all wrong.

"I can't do that! I need to see Christine."

Zemma nods. "I should have explained things a little differently. Gabriel, you may be the single greatest asset the United States has for homeland security. I can't tell you more than that until you begin training, but you have to understand, this is intense, critical work. You'll be helping to keep the peace and disenfranchise the enemies while our citizens are sleeping in their beds. It isn't a fun club to belong to. It isn't a frolic in fantasyland. This is serious. Millions of lives are counting on our work, whether they know it or not. It takes big sacrifices to do a job this crucial. You have to take this all into account, not just how much you want to get with your girlfriend."

I should have known. Why would someone expect me to be important and powerful without taking away the only thing in the world that I want.

"Damn it," I say.

Zemma places her hand gently on my arm. "Sorry, Agent. I know it isn't easy. Why don't you go home and talk to your girl? I'll come back for you Saturday night. That should give you enough time to get things in order."

"Isn't that only three days?"

Zemma shrugs. "It only took God six days to make the universe. I think you can do what you need to in three."

"Who said I believe in God?"

"Three days, Agent."

And I'm back in my apartment, alone.

40

Christine

The ringing of my cell made me jump. I followed the ringing into my room, where my purse was laying on the floor. What felt like a couple minutes of rummaging passed until I found the phone, just before it went to voicemail.

"Hello?" I asked, not even checking who was calling.

"Christine."

That was all it took for tears to form at the corners of my eyes.

"I'm so happy you're all right!" I said, not even hiding the high-pitched emotion in my voice.

"God, Christine. I'm so sorry about everything. I just want to see you so bad. Can I come over?"

"Yes," I cried into the phone.

"I'll be there in two seconds."

He clicked off the phone and I stuffed mine back into my purse.

Leo tapped at my doorframe. "Everything okay?"

I nodded and wiped at my eyes with the back of my hands. "Gabriel's coming over."

Leo walked over to my nightstand and grabbed the Kleenex box. Kneeling down next to me, he offered me a few tissues.

"I'm sure you two have a lot to talk about. I shouldn't be around when he gets here."

He was right, but I still didn't want him to leave.

"Don't go too far away," I sniffed, starting to pull myself together again.

"I won't," he assured me. He stood to go but crouched down again. He squeezed my shoulder. "Listen, I know this is really hard. It wasn't easy for me, either. If there was some way I could make this better for you, I would."

My chin prepared to quiver again, so I grabbed Leo and hugged him close. He didn't hesitate in closing his arms around me like a wall of stability in the craziness that had become my life. He had a knack for doing just the right thing at the right time. I guess that's why he made a great dream agent.

Holding Leo calmed me down. I didn't want to let go, but I knew it wouldn't be good if he was still there when Gabriel showed up. In control of quivery chins and leaky tear ducts, I gave him an extra squeeze and pulled away.

I couldn't find the right words, but I could see Leo understood clearer than if I'd said anything.

"I'll be close," he said and left.

I took a few deep breaths and pulled myself up from the floor. The situation wouldn't be any better if Gabriel found me huddled on the floor like a broken mess.

Dream Girl

I straightened my shirt and smoothed my shorts, hoping I'd look stronger than I felt. The knock came at the door just as I walked out of the bedroom.

41

Gabriel

Christine looks so tired. I notice that right away. But she doesn't look any less beautiful. All I want is to throw myself into her arms and get lost in her kisses, but I don't deserve that. Not after I ran out on her before. Not since it was Leo, not me, who was able to help her in the dreamworld. There will be no kisses unless she decides to give them. From the look in her eye, that is the last thought in her mind.

Her lips curve into a shaky smile. She doesn't want to cry, but her eyes are already red. Still, she pulls me through the door and squeezes me with all she's worth. Her face nestles into my neck and the cherry-sweet smell of her shampoo fills my nostrils. For the moment, the weight on my shoulders dissolves and I'm home again, in the only place I want to belong.

I think she's crying, but she doesn't make a sound. I'm happy to hold her as long as she wants me to.

Finally, her lips brush against my neck as she speaks.

"Things are so messed up."

I separate myself from her arms so I can look at

her. There are tears clinging under her eyes. I brush them away with my thumb as gently as I can.

"I know," I say. "They want me to go away and join them. They think I have these amazing abilities and I should get into training immediately. It sounds ridiculous to say that out loud." I run my fingers through my hair. How could I have believed Zemma? The only amazing powers I have are to wreck things. If millions of people are relying on me to keep them safe, they'll be bitterly disappointed.

Christine shakes her head. "It isn't ridiculous. You're capable of more than you give yourself credit for."

"I ran when you needed me because I was too weak to help you. Who knew I was capable of that?"

Christine waves her hands, brushing off what I just said, but I see the confusion in her eyes. Whether she'll admit it or not, I did hurt her.

"A lot has happened since then," she says.

I can't argue with that.

"Are you okay?" I ask. "This chick kept telling me you were safe with Leo, but are you really all right?"

Her lips curve into a small smile. "Yes. Leo's been talking with me about everything. Turns out you aren't the only one they want to recruit."

Am I hearing this right?

A flutter of selfish hope forms in my chest. Is it possible we could try this insanity out, together? She must know what I'm thinking.

"They didn't tell you," she says.

"What?"

She grabs my hand and laces her fingers with mine. With a gentle tug, she leads me over to the couch. We sit down and collapse into each other. I can make out an indistinct reflection of us in the dark television. Her head on my shoulder, my head resting on top of hers, we look like a regular couple. No one would suspect we were talking about secret government agencies and the possibility of joining one.

She positions our joined hands on her thigh and outlines my fingers with her other hand as she explains. If she's trying to distract me, she's doing one hell of a good job.

"We won't be together if we both join. It's not group training; it's one on one with a mentor. And," she takes a deep breath, "it can take years."

Things have gotten worse again.

"How convenient. Zemma left that part out," I say through gritted teeth.

"Zemma?"

"Yeah, she's the one who explained things to me. She said she'd train me, not that she'd be the only person around."

"Do you want to do it?" she asks.

"She didn't tell me the truth," I say. She was certainly convinced I was some kind of prize. I guess she would say whatever it took to entice me. So why did Leo tell Christine?

"Forget the truth," Christine urges, still tracing our fingers. "Did you want to do it when she told you about it?"

"I don't know. Sorta. I mean, she was a smooth talker. She made it sound like I was really special and I'd be some amazing asset for the government. It sounded important, but I wasn't sure I could do it."

"But you wanted to try?"

"She was so sure of me and I liked what she was saying. Yeah, I wanted to be what she described."

"If I wasn't here, would you have come back?"

She knows the answer to that, but I'm not going to play along with this game.

"You are here. There's no point wondering about if you weren't. I'd probably be dead. You and Leo were the only ones standing between me and that psycho guy."

She stiffens when I mention psycho guy. "But," she pauses and traces our fingers faster. "I think she's right. I think you are really important. It explains why this has been happening to you for so long. Just keep that in mind."

And there it is. She wants me to go. She won't come out and say it, but I know that's what she means. The surprising thing is how much it hurts to realize this. It's not like she's trying to get rid of me because she doesn't like me. The energy from her hands, where we're touching, assures me that she's still interested. But still, she's willing to let me go for a perceived greater good. It's incredibly noble but intensely painful as well. I don't know if I could do the same if our roles were reversed.

"Yeah," I say, trying not to choke on the lump in my throat. "It's something to consider."

"I didn't say that right," she backpedals. "I mean, I

know you're really important. Without any of this. The dreamworld isn't what makes you special. You do that all on your own."

I put my free hand over hers to still the incessant tracing. Her words fill up the aching pain she'd unintentionally inflicted and make it shine. This is more complicated than anything I could imagine. Visiting the dreamworld suddenly seems clear-cut compared to the decisions I have to make now.

I can't restrain myself any longer.

I keep my eyes on her perfect, pink lips and lean in.

She closes her eyes and I, finally, place my lips on hers. It is a kiss like no other. There is an exquisite rush of despair, passion, understanding and loss. I realize now that no matter what we choose, we lose. If I go, I lose Christine. If I don't go, I lose the opportunity to discover the most mysterious part of myself.

I have three days to figure out which is the loss I can live with.

42

Christine

There was so much I wanted to ask, but it was too late. All the unasked questions had combined to form a new question, bigger than any of them on their own. Now, we couldn't be bothered to figure out what had happened in the past, there was only one thing: would either of us go or would we stay?

Wrapped in Gabriel's desperate kisses, I didn't know what to do anymore. He was electrifying in the same way that Leo was calming. With Leo, I thought I knew what to do. With Gabriel, I didn't have a clue.

Zemma had told him he was important, an asset to the government. Even when Leo told me about it, he didn't seem to believe Gabriel would choose not to recruit.

Leo thought I was special, but not in the same way as Gabriel. As much as I'd denied it, Gabriel was probably right. I had never been aware of the dreamworld before I'd met him. If he had somehow launched me into the dreamworld, he was powerful. Clearly, the government wanted him. Apart from me, he had no reason not to go. But did I have any business even considering recruitment? I didn't really have any ability. They might think that now, but not once I started training and it became obvious I couldn't do anything. What would happen then? Would they kick me out and erase my brain anyway? Maybe joining would only prolong the inevitable.

I pulled away from Gabriel. "We can't do this," I said.

Gabriel's eyes looked disappointed, but not surprised.

"I thought you might say that."

"It's not you," I said, twining my fingers into his. "It's all of this. It feels like saying goodbye. I can't stand it."

Gabriel leaned his forehead against mine.

"I never expected to be in a situation like this," he said.

"I know."

"I have until Saturday night to decide."

"What?" I stared into Gabriel's eyes.

"Zemma said she'd come back for me on Saturday night."

As if on cue, my cell started ringing with the ringtone I programmed for Tiffany.

"Sorry, I'll be right back."

"I didn't expect you to answer!" Tiffany said.

"It isn't the best time," I replied.

"Is Leo still there?" There was no mistaking the excitement in her voice.

"No, Gabriel is."

"What, can't they be in the same room together? I thought they were friends."

"They are friends. Leo had something to do."

"I'll bet," Tiffany said.

I tried to end the call. "Listen, can I—"

"I think Leo has the hots for you. He can't stand to see you with Gabriel. That's why he left."

I sighed. "Thanks for the analysis."

"I'm not kidding. Don't tell me you didn't notice how he was looking at you. That guy would do anything for you. I'm so glad I stumbled in on your clandestine rendezvous to meet him."

"Can I call you— "

"No, this is really quick. I've already talked to a ton of people since I left you and my parents are hosting a going away party for me this Saturday."

"What?" Crazy news was coming at me from all directions. There was no way to keep up.

Tiffany laughed. "Leo isn't my type, but he's definitely cute in his own way. No one can blame you for getting a little flustered."

"Would you stop it? Gabriel's here, I told you."

"Eh. Whatever. It's not like you two are married. You're well within your rights to play the field."

"I'm hanging up now," I said.

"No you aren't!" she yelled. "You're coming to my party on Saturday. We're going to leave the following Saturday."

"What?" I said again.

She laughed. "My parents are on board. Marcel

said the sooner we go, the longer we can stay. We don't have to come back until school starts. It's going to be amazing!"

"I can't believe this," I mumbled.

"Believe it!" Tiffany said. "And you better not forget my party. It's *this* Saturday. Maybe you should write it down."

"Funny."

"Okay, I'll let you get back to your guys, Lovergirl."

"I'm going to kill you."

"Au revoir!" She ended the call before I could say another word.

I slammed the phone onto my nightstand with a less than satisfying "clunk." The walls were closing in on me.

I headed back to the living room to find Gabriel sitting on the couch with his head in his hands.

"What's wrong?" I asked, even though "what's right?" would have been a more appropriate question.

Gabriel looked up and no words were needed. Something bad had happened while I was talking to Tiffany.

43

Gabriel

W hat's wrong?" she asks. A question I should be able to answer but don't know if I can. How can I explain what just happened while she was answering her phone? One second I was sitting on the couch watching her walk to her room, the next I was sucked into the dreamworld without any notice. I hadn't even fallen asleep.

Zemma appeared, before my eyes, to deliver one brief, chilling message. "Gabriel, there's been a security breach. Apparently, the traitor wasn't acting alone. Your physical location has been compromised. You have to leave. Agent Bonaventure is in your location. He's going to pick you up and bring you to the agency. You won't need anything. Don't worry."

And she was gone. No chance to ask questions. No time to process what the hell she was talking about, but I do understand one thing: They're taking me, whether I want to go or not.

I look at Christine, standing wide-eyed across the room. I have no idea where to begin.

A knock at the door makes us both jump.

"Christine, it's me. Open up!" says a male voice laced with urgency.

Christine rushes to the door and pulls it open, revealing her hawk-nosed hero. Leo, to the rescue, again. But what is he doing in our real world? And how does he know where to find us?

"What's going on?" she asks, looking from him to me. She doesn't seem surprised that he's here, and the realization clutches my heart like an iron fist.

Leo frowns and I can see the genuine frustration in his eyes.

"It appears Brett Lawrence wasn't acting as our only rebel agent," he says. "Our location has been hacked by at least one other rebel, presumably because they know your dream frequencies are being monitored now."

"Speak English, Leo," Christine interrupts with authority, like she's talking to a long-time friend.

"We have to leave," he says.

Christine and Leo stare at each other for a long moment. Their eyes seem to exchange more information than I could share with words in a few days' time.

Finally, Christine turns back to me. She doesn't know what to say.

"Zemma said Agent Bonaventure was coming to get me," I say.

Leo nods. "Agent Leo Bonaventure at your service."

44

Christine

W e have to leave" thundered like an endless echo through the corridors of my mind. It's the sort of crisis that seems thrilling in a book or movie, but there is no thrill when it becomes a personal reality.

We had to leave. *I* had to leave. The trouble was, even though I understood the meaning of the words, I didn't actually know what to do.

I turned to Gabriel to see how he was processing the news. He sat on the couch, hands folded between his knees, staring straight at me. He didn't look like he was about to go anywhere.

I noticed the light pressure of Leo's fingertips on my shoulder. I turned back to him and saw a flicker of sorrow in his eyes.

"None of this is going right," he said quietly.

"What do we do?" I asked.

He never got a chance to answer.

45

Gabriel

The door explodes into the room. It slams into Leo's back and sends him sprawling into Christine. They both crash to the ground. I leap up to get Christine, but I'm stopped in my tracks by an all-too-familiar laugh.

Standing in the doorway is Anime chick and her giant sidekick. He looks even larger and more menacing when framed by the narrow doorframe. But it's neither of them who are laughing.

My hands clench automatically and adrenalin surges through my veins. I don't know what will happen, but I do know that it's all going to end, one way or another, right now.

Finally, the little weasel pushes his way between the two henchmen and crosses the threshold. For once, he isn't wearing his stupid trademark sunglasses.

Leo scrambles up, off of Christine, and just as Leo turns to face the guy, he gets pistol-whipped before any of us see it coming. I hear his nose pop just before blood gushes out and he staggers back on his knees. Christine gasps and her eyes widen in horror.

"We meet again," Brett says, looking at me and

twisting his lips into a snarly smile.

"You're out of your mind!" I shout at him.

"On the contrary," he says, "I'm very clearheaded. You are the only thing standing in my way, so I've come to get rid of you, properly."

He holds up a black device, the same thing he hit Leo in the face with. I thought it was a pistol, but now I see it's some other thing. I have a vague memory that I've seen one before. I'm not sure what it does, but it's definitely some kind of weapon, if only for smashing noses.

"At least tell me what I'm in the way of," I say, stalling for time now.

He sighs impatiently but indulges me.

"Let me say this slowly so you can understand," he taunts. "You are the fabled son of Agent Chase, a god among men. He is the most famous, most respected agent there ever was. Everyone expects you to be just as amazing. They want to hand the agency over to you on a golden platter, even though you know nothing about it and have less training ability than our lowest-ranked recruits."

I see where this is heading, so I cut him off.

"Really? A power play? That's all this is? Well, you're in luck. I don't want anything to do with your beloved agency. Go ahead and take it over. I don't care."

Brett narrows his eyes. "This is the Federal government we're talking about," he hisses. "It gets what it wants, and right now, Uncle Sam wants you. It doesn't matter if you're willing or not. There's only one way out of this now." He waggles the device in his hand as he raises it in my direction. "Just think of it as a favor I'm doing for you. You can thank me later."

"I really don't think—" I fumble for words that can convince a psychopath to find his lost sanity. I try to speak faster and more eloquently, because I see Leo preparing to attack. Unfortunately, Brett notices too. He spins toward Leo and holds the device inches from his broken beak. Leo's nose is still bleeding heavily, but his eyes look calm. He's either one hell of an actor or more of a badass than I'd given him credit for.

"Are you planning to overthrow Zemma?" Leo asks without so much as a waver in his voice.

My Zemma? I didn't realize she was running the show. I wish I'd had time to get some real answers.

"Shut him up!" Brett yells, and the giant guy hastens to Leo's side. Leo stands up quickly and holds up his hands. "Stand down, Agent!"

Apparently, he is a badass.

The giant doesn't look as sure of himself as Brett does and Leo jumps on it.

"That's an order!"

"Your rank means nothing here," Brett shouts.

"Zemma won't stand for this. She'll have you rotting in Federal prison, with a permanent mind-block, before you know what hit you. These two won't do much better, unless they rethink this insurrection right now."

Tension crackles through the air as we wait to see if Anime chick and the giant will cave to the pressure or if they've truly cast their lot in with Brett.

It doesn't take long for their decision. The giant pulls out a black device and lunges at Leo. In the same instant, Christine screams and I throw myself toward Brett. I see the surprise in his blue eyes as I zero in on my target. Every muscle in my body has been aching for the opportunity to pay this guy back for everything about the dreamworld that's ruined my life and Christine's. I will tear this bastard apart if I have to. He can't trap me in mental Jell-O this time.

My fist connects with his throat and I feel him crumple beneath me. We topple to the ground and it feels like we're falling in slow motion. There is no confidence in his eyes, only fear, and I realize I've finally got the upper hand. We're on my turf now.

46

Christine

I thought things were beyond hope when Brett broke Leo's nose, but things managed to degenerate further.

The big guy came after Leo, and they struggled as I lay on the ground gaping in horror at what was happening in Daria's living room. The guy had some sort of device with metal prongs that he seemed determined to push into Leo's neck. Leo, despite being less than half the guy's size, managed to hold his own. I was watching the two of them when Gabriel came into my periphery. I turned slightly to see him rushing Brett. That's when I noticed the girl making her move toward me, a pronged device in her hand, too.

Since most of the action was taking place in front of the door, there was nowhere to run. My options were to stand my ground against a government agent or try to lock myself in the bathroom. I sprang to my feet and decided I'd have to stay and fight, as best I could. She was already within striking distance. I tried to swipe the device from her hand, but my wrist brushed against the prongs in the process. I jumped back with a squeal. The prongs had burned a rising welt in my skin.

"Just let me do this," she said. "It doesn't hurt when it's done properly."

Somehow, I didn't believe her.

"No!" I screamed, like I'd been taught in a rape prevention presentation we'd had in school.

The girl actually rolled her eyes and lunged at me with the device aimed at my neck.

My body tensed in anticipation of the burn, but it didn't come.

Leo, still grappling with the big guy, managed to kick the girl in the knee, just enough to knock her off balance.

"Christine, run!" Leo yelled, as the girl crashed into Gabriel and Brett. I did have a clear path to the door now, but how could I leave them like this?

"Now!" Leo commanded.

The girl was already scrambling back to her feet, but I noticed she'd dropped her device. Before I could even think, I snatched it off the floor then turned to push her back down. Surprised, she went down easily and I jabbed the prongs into the side of her neck. Her eyes widened for a split second before they rolled back and she collapsed.

Adrenaline surged through my body. I'd actually taken down an agent, but I didn't get much of a chance to feel powerful. The big guy noticed and shoved Leo against the wall with a thump that knocked Daria's framed poster down.

He was on me in two strides and plucked the device out of my hands like I was nothing. He stood a good head taller than me and was built like a refrigerator. He spun me around and pinned my arms behind my back. Squirming was pointless. There was no chance I could do anything to this guy.

With my back to him, I was now facing Gabriel and Brett. There was no way to describe them other than they were locked in a death match. Both of them looked wild and desperate, fighting for their lives. An icy shard of horror lodged in my heart, causing me to shiver. As long as I live, I will never be able to forget the raw hatred in their eyes as they punched and snarled at each other.

Suddenly, the big guy released his grip on me and toppled to the ground. Leo stood behind him, brandishing a black device.

"We've got to get out of here now!" he said, his skin looking extra pale compared to the blood streaming down the lower half of his face.

"What about—" I started to turn my head to Gabriel and Brett, but Leo shook his head and grabbed my hand.

"You first," he said as he tugged me firmly toward the door.

Feeling Leo's fingers around mine gave me a sense of security. He'd just managed to take down refrigerator man. I trusted his judgment and followed his lead.

We ran, together, out of the apartment and out of the building. He led me toward the back of the parking lot, finally stopping at a black car with black-tinted windows. He fumbled a key out of his back pocket and unlocked the car.

"Where are we going?" I asked.

"Nowhere. We'll sit tight here while I call Zemma. She can keep those two deactivated and get ready for Brett."

I burned with more questions, but it wasn't the right time.

I crawled into the passenger seat and he closed the door behind me. By the time he'd come around to the driver's side, he was already talking to Zemma.

I didn't listen as he quickly filled her in. Instead, I tucked my hands under my knees and tried to process what had just happened. My eyes strayed, unfocused, toward the apartment building where Brett and Gabriel were still fighting. The whole situation was so bizarre it hardly seemed real.

"Holy shit!" exclaimed Leo, snapping me back to attention.

"What?" I asked, fearing the worst.

"I look like hell!" he said, catching sight of himself in the rearview mirror.

"You should be at the hospital," I said. "Doesn't it hurt?"

"Don't have time to think about it," he said. "I've gotta go back in."

"No way," I said. "I thought Zemma could take care of it."

"She can take care of those two traitors, but not Brett. He's too advanced for her to pull him into the dreamworld while he's awake. I've got to go in there and get him with this," he pulled the black device out of his pocket.

"What is that thing?" I asked.

"It shocks the nervous system into a state of unconsciousness that mimics the dream state, allowing the agents to take over. Which is what I should be doing to Brett right now."

I put my hand on his arm, "I don't want you to go back there alone."

"There's no one else to go with," he said.

"There's me."

"I'm not putting you in harm's way again. I don't want to leave you here either, but it's the better of the two options."

"You're already hurt."

"Looks worse than it is," he said.

"Liar."

"No one dies of a broken nose."

"Who knows how much blood you've lost. You're weaker than normal."

"I appreciate your concern, really, but this is my job. I can handle it." He put his hand on top of mine and gave it a quick squeeze.

"I promise I'll be right back." He hopped out of the car and jogged back into the apartment without so much as a backward glance.

47

Gabriel

I never should have let you go."

I hear the voice, but I can't place it right away. I have a vague feeling that I was just in the middle of something else but can't think of what.

Why can't I see anything?

I open my eyes. Yeah, that explains some things. Zemma is standing in front of me, and she looks pissed as hell.

"What's going on?" I ask.

Zemma crosses her arms and holds her head higher.

"You're not going back there," she says. "It's too dangerous for everyone. You can't go running around untrained anymore, and that's how it is."

"What? You're holding me captive now?"

"I'm keeping your ass safe," she snaps. "Brett meant business today, and now we know he wasn't acting alone. We don't know how many more agents he was subverting, but your location isn't secure anymore. You're staying here."

Things aren't adding up. I realize I'm in the

dreamworld again because I'm hazy on what I was doing just before I got here. If the aches all over my body are any indication, I was either working very hard or getting the shit kicked out of me. I put that together with her comment about Brett and everything snaps into place.

"What happened to Christine?" I ask.

"Agent Bonaventure is very skilled. She's still with him, but I can't say who is protecting whom right now." She smirks and I remember how Brett broke Leo's nose.

"Is she all right?" Adrenaline starts surging again.

Zemma puts up her hands. "I shouldn't be joking with you. Yes, she's completely unharmed. She escorted Agent Bonaventure to the ER. That's where they are now."

"And where are we?"

"That's a trick question. You're in the dream state and I'm at headquarters."

"So where's my body? Is Brett decimating it as we speak?"

"No. Agent Bonaventure neutralized him. We have him and the other two traitors in a dream state lockdown. I believe you're at the ER now, too, until additional agents can get there to escort you to headquarters."

"You know, none of that really makes sense," I say.

She smiles apologetically. "Let me rephrase. You and Agent Bonaventure are getting checked out at the ER. Christine is with you both. By the time you're discharged, two agents will be there to bring you to headquarters."

"So I have no say in this anymore?" I ask, remembering what Brett had said about the government getting what it wants.

"I'm afraid not," Zemma says, her tone softening. "You've been drafted in the United States Agency of Dream Work. It's a matter of national security."

I don't see how I have anything to do with national security, but I have more pressing concerns.

"Is Christine drafted, too?"

"With all due respect, Agent, she is not nearly as important as you. Although she has become privy to classified information, we can easily remedy that, should she choose to remain civilian."

"In other words," I say, my heart beginning to race. "If she doesn't choose to enlist, you'll kill her."

Zemma's eyes get big and then she laughs.

"God, no!" she exclaims. "We aren't the mafia." She composes herself and continues, but a smile still tugs at her lips. "We're more like a sci-fi movie. We can erase things, repress things; she'll go about her business and never realize she met us at all."

"What?" I say quieter than I expected. My throat is suddenly very dry.

"Don't worry," Zemma says. "It doesn't hurt. You'll learn all about it in training, so why don't we leave it at that?"

There is so much I want to know, but at the same time, I don't want to know it. I hear Zemma's words forming a loop in my brain. *She'll never realize she met us.* Does "us" include me?

Now I know I have no choice whether I become an agent or not, but the tension is even stronger. Christine still has a decision to make and I'm torn over which option is best for her. Selfishly, of course, I don't want to lose her, but she still has a chance to go back to a normal life. The normal life I stole from her somehow. I guess that would be justice. She wouldn't remember that I messed up her life and I would no longer have the most wonderful girl in the world. But neither would Leo, I realize with a jolt of satisfaction. But it isn't up to me to decide a path for Christine. She's gotta make this one herself. The hardest part will be letting her.

48

Christine

Sitting in the ER with two guys I'd come to care for was not my idea of a good time. Even though I knew both of them would be okay, there was a lot riding on the outcome anyway. And I sat, alone, in the waiting room because I didn't think it would be fair to sit at the bedside of only one of them. I didn't think hospital staff would appreciate me playing musical rooms either. So I sat alone with a year-old *People* magazine in my hands, trying not to listen to the groaning and sighing of the others in the waiting room.

I couldn't stop imagining the attack in Daria's apartment. There was an agent there now. She was supposed to protect things while we were gone, since the door didn't exactly close anymore. Maintenance was going to love that. They'd also love the blood stains on the carpet. And the crack in the plaster from Leo's head slamming into it. Dream agents. What might I be getting myself into?

I thought back to the conversation Leo and I had had, face to face, before everything had gone to hell. Despite what had just happened, I had a decision to make. To stay involved but isolated from Gabriel and Leo for training, or bow out now and forget the whole mess. Since the ambush, the latter option didn't seem quite so horrible. But could I really give up both of them now?

If I was being honest, I hadn't known either of them very long at all, but we'd already lived lifetimes together.

My stomach growled and I remembered I hadn't eaten anything since I didn't know when. I tossed the unopened magazine into the empty chair next to me and absently got up to find a vending machine. I wandered down the supposedly sterile hallways, hoping for a sign. For vending and for what to do with my life.

It wasn't so long ago that I was excited to start senior year with Tiffany. I wanted to take classes, travel the world, meet guys and figure my life out along the way. Apparently, the common thread between then and now was not knowing what to do with myself for the big picture. Plenty of things sounded cool but nothing really got me fired up. What about dream work? Leo wasn't able to tell me exactly what that meant, but it was obviously dangerous.

Why couldn't someone just tell me what to do?

I turned the corner and found a vending machine. A woman holding a baby stood in front of it, examining the contents. The baby kept reaching her hands up to the woman's face, and the woman patiently patted them back down so she could see the machine.

Cute, I thought, watching the baby's untiring quest

to touch her mother's face.

Then the vision struck me like a physical blow. I reeled back against the wall, heart racing. In my mind's eye, I saw another baby and mother, the one from the dreamworld. *Save my baby.* She'd given me the directive as clear as anything, but I hadn't acted. I didn't know what she meant. But the floodgates were opening. I could feel myself standing on the verge of understanding. Images flooded my brain faster and faster. The woman's face. The baby's hands. The desolate street. The baby's face. Gabriel's face. The baby's eyes. Gabriel's eyes. *Gabriel's eyes.*

Oh.

My.

God.

I gasped and the vending mother glanced in my direction with a thin veil of annoyance over her expression. But it didn't matter. Sound bites from my conversations with Gabriel and Leo filtered through my mind like a file folder downloading into my brain.

The woman finally punched the buttons for her selection and a bag of salty snacks clunked into the tray. She bent down to retrieve it and walked past me without another glance, but I couldn't stop staring at her and the baby.

"Thank you," I whispered to her back as they disappeared down the hall. Maybe I wasn't really thanking her, but somehow she had put the pieces all together for me.

I turned away from the vending machine, hunger

forgotten, and walked back toward the ER waiting room with purpose. But, I wouldn't go back to my uncomfortable seat and an expired magazine. There was a bedside I needed to sit at.

I'd made my decision.

49

Gabriel

I open my eyes and see the garish white hospital all around me. Shit. Zemma wasn't kidding. I look down to see the IV flowing into my veins. What it's there for, I don't know. I do know I feel worse than I ever have. That bastard really took the piss out of me. I hope he's lying in the morgue right about now.

A pretty nurse strolls in and smiles when she sees me.

"Oh, hello Mr. Gray. How are you feeling?" she asks. She leans over the bed a bit and examines the IV bag.

"Like shit," I answer.

She makes a happy-person-playing-sad face, but she smells really good, like bubble gum and coconut, so it doesn't bother me.

"I know. You've been through quite an accident. Do you want more pain meds?"

Do I? Why not? I see Christine is not beside me. For a moment, I picture her draped over Leo in his bed, dabbing his forehead with a cool cloth. Why would she be doing such a thing in an ER room? I don't know. But that's what I picture, and it makes me want the strongest pain meds available. In high doses.

I nod slightly and notice the muscles in my neck feel like iron rods.

"Okay, I'll be right back with that. Do you need anything else? Something to drink or some crackers?"

"No thanks. I'm good," I reply, and she disappears.

I stare at the ceiling and try not to wonder why there's a brownish stain up there.

I look up when someone walks in. Expecting the nurse, I'm surprised to see a guy and girl I don't recognize, although the way they carry themselves is familiar.

"We're here to escort you back to headquarters, Agent Gray," says the girl.

"Are you going to wait for them to remove the IV, or do agents do that themselves?" I've had it with this whole agency by now. I'm not in the mood to make nice.

The girl looks grim.

"I'm sorry about these circumstances. Would you prefer if we stayed in the waiting room?"

I glance down at my ill-fitting hospital gown. It doesn't get more personal than this.

"Whatever," I say. "I belong to you now, right?"

The girl glances uneasily at the guy.

"It's our job to keep this from happening again," he says.

"Right. Since you did such a great job last time."

Oh yeah. Me and that guy are going to be good buddies.

"Listen, you don't have to be an asshole," he whispers, but the girl hears him and jabs him in the ribs. It makes me smile. Maybe I really am an asshole.

"We'll wait until you're discharged," the girl says. "We just wanted you to know we're here now."

"Yippee," I say, and they walk out the door. Maybe I'm lucky and this guy is on the mutinous side, too, so he'll get a chance to take a shot at me when I get out. Never can tell with this upstanding government agency. Nothing but the best for them.

After awhile, the nurse comes back and turns up the happy juice in my IV.

Ahhh. Nice nurse.

"Blah, blah, blah," she says and smiles.

I smile back. So warm and fuzzy.

Maybe I'll just stay here. Forever.

50

Christine

"I know what I'm going to do," I said as I gripped the edge of Leo's bed. I tried to ignore the tape on his nose and the stray specks of dried blood on his face that weren't successfully wiped clean.

I could actually see him steel himself for what I was going to say. He definitely knew what he wanted me to do. Confidence mingled with fear, but I was sure he'd agree with my decision.

"Okay," he said, calm as ever. "What's your decision?"

The nurse came in. Perfectly scripted, like a play.

"All right, Mr. Bonaventure, I've got your discharge papers here,"

"Could we just have a couple minutes?" I said, turning to her in frustration.

"But you can just take these and—"

"Yeah, thanks. But we need to sort something out first. Just a couple more minutes. We'll get out after that."

The nurse probably didn't get many people wanting to put off discharge, but she nodded, like I was nuts, handed the papers to Leo and left.

"Wow," he said quietly. "I guess you have made up your mind."

"Yes, and I need to say it now." I took a deep breath. "I'm recruiting."

Time stopped.

A million thoughts burst to the surface of Leo's blue eyes, but he masked them all before I could get a good read on them.

His stoicism was impressive.

Finally. Carefully. He replied.

"Your mind is made up," he said.

"No going back," I replied.

"May I ask what made you decide?"

"It's a crazy thing, really."

He nodded. "It has to be. Nothing particularly sane when it comes to dream work."

"Well," I said, perching on the edge of his bed. He scooted over as much as he could to give me more room. I angled myself so I was sitting and facing him, for the most part. "A few things happened to me in the dreamworld that I haven't told you or Gabriel about."

Leo tensed but I put my hand on his knee to calm him.

"Not bad things, but I think, if I'm reading this right, you're going to need me in the agency. At least, Gabriel is."

"Okay," he said, waiting for me to go on.

"Well, there's a woman I've run into a couple times, when I'm by myself. She's always in a house, at night, and hers is the only house with any lights on. She stands by the window with a baby. The first time, she held up the baby for me to look at. It was a really cute baby but a bizarre thing to do. Anyway, I forgot about it and life went on. But, the second time, she told me to 'save her baby.' That was terrifying, but I still forgot about it until now. I saw a woman with a baby in the hallway, and all these images came together, and things I've talked about with you and Gabriel and it hit me, Leo. Gabriel is that baby. Their eyes are exactly the same. I'm in this for a reason. I have to stay in."

Leo was shocked enough that the incredulity showed on his battered face.

"Do you realize what this means?" he asked.

"Probably not," I said honestly.

"Christine, I think you may have been summoned after all, but not by a current agent."

As was becoming customary, I didn't follow, but I could see Leo was talking this one out as it occurred to him.

"When Agent Chase was murdered, his wife and child disappeared. Frankly, the agency didn't mind much. Our condolences were formally offered to the widow but, beyond that, there was no reason for further contact. Now we know Gabriel's mother placed him for adoption. The last time she saw him, Gabriel was a baby. As the wife of the most talented dream agent in the history of the organization, it's possible she could have acquired some skills of her own. If nothing else, a mother's love has been known to do impossible things.

Maybe she sensed her son was in trouble, and found you because you were..." he faltered for the slightest second, "...close to him."

It was so incredibly insane that it had to have some truth to it.

"Right," I said, pretending I'd come to that exact conclusion myself. Well, I'd figured Gabriel's mother wanted me to help him somehow. Close enough.

"This is big," Leo said. "Zemma's going to want a team on this ASAP."

"Ah!" I interjected, forming a new plan and the confidence to go with it, on the fly. "About Zemma, I have a condition for recruitment."

A small smile tugged at the corners of Leo's lips.

"By all means," he said.

"I will not train with anyone other than you."

He couldn't mask his shock on that one.

"But I'm not on the current training—"

"I don't care. If you don't train me, I'd rather be erased. And I don't think anyone will want me erased now." I was bluffing, really. I didn't know if anyone cared where Gabriel's mother was, but I felt like I had something to bargain with, so I seized it.

"But there are far more qualified trainers," he said quietly, not meeting my eyes.

I weighed my words carefully, not entirely sure how to validate my own demand.

"We're the right team," I said finally.

He squinted as if trying to read the fine print in my eyes.

I stared back, suddenly feeling self-conscious.

Then tentatively, so tentatively, he placed his hand over mine.

I leaned in and rested my head on his chest. I could hear his heart thumping as wildly as my own.

"One problem," he whispered into the top of my head.

"What?"

"When do you turn eighteen?"

I sat up in shock.

"You're kidding me," I gasped. "Isn't there any way around it?"

"Only if your parents are willing to sign you away to the US government."

There was no way that would fly with my parents.

"My birthday isn't until March. Are you seriously suggesting that I can't recruit until then? Can't you do something?"

Leo looked at me with calm eyes, but I could see the wheels turning.

"There might be a loophole, but I'll have to talk to Zemma." He frowned. "There's a good chance you might have to wait until March, though."

How could this be possible? Just when I'd decided what to do, I still had to sit around waiting?

"So what does that mean? You're all going to leave me and I just get to twiddle my thumbs until my birthday?"

"No," said Leo. "I'm not going to leave you. You're still in my protection, remember?"

"What if Zemma changes her mind? What if no one thinks I'm worth recruiting by March?"

"This might be for the best," Leo said. "I can use the time to work on becoming a trainer."

It sounded reasonable, but I couldn't shake the feeling that everything was slipping from my grasp.

"Why does everything have to be so complicated?" I complained.

"It wouldn't be worthwhile if it wasn't," Leo offered.

I sighed and rested my head on his chest again. Listening to the soothing rhythm of his heart, a new idea popped into my head.

"I have one more demand," I said into his sternum.

"Anything," he answered.

"You have to stay with me while you heal and you have to take me to Tiffany's going-away party Saturday."

He laughed as much as he could stand with a newly broken nose.

"I think that can be arranged."

51

Gabriel

My eyes open and I see I'm still in the hospital. Who knows what time it is? Or what day it is, for that matter. And when will I get out of here? Not that I really want to. Getting out means the draft. I wonder if there's any way I can dodge those clowns in the waiting room. Maybe the nurse will help me slip out the back door or something.

I sit up to assess my bodily damages.

Sore.

But not unbearable.

What's a guy gotta do to take a piss around here?

I move to swing my legs over the bed when I notice a piece of paper near my knee. Normally, I wouldn't care about a hospital paper, but this appears to be covered in handwriting. Like a letter. Not like a prescription.

I lean forward to pick up it. Yeah, that stings a little, but I'm too intrigued to be bothered with a little pain.

Dear Gabriel,

There's so much to say and no time to say it. I wish things were turning out differently.

Anyway, I want you to know some things.

First, I'm really confused about us. I don't think we were given a fair chance to get things off the ground, but I do know I'm connected to you. Always and forever. And I think that's a good thing. But I also know circumstances don't allow us to be normal, now or even in the foreseeable future. Leo told me Zemma is recruiting you immediately, and he also told me training can last up to three years. And you can't be in contact with anyone. So that sort of cuts us off right there.

Second, that's not the end.

Really? It sounds like it to me. Suddenly, I have a lot more pain than a broken body.

I've decided to recruit too, but I can't until March. I know that means you'll probably finish way ahead of me, but we'll both come out in the same reality in the end, however long that takes.

Third, I'm sorry I'm writing you this stupid note instead of sitting beside you in that horrible hospital room. I hope you understand, but I just can't do it. I'm afraid that if I see you, I won't go through with it. Something happens when we're too close. I don't think straight anymore.

Okay, at least she remembers that. Maybe there's hope after all.

See? There I go. Anyway. I can't tell you right now, but I think the Agency needs me. I think you need me in the Agency, too.

That said, I guess I just wanted to say that you and I, Gabriel & Christine, are suspended, guilt free, until we both come out the other side of this crazy thing and can start over in a new normal.

I hope you don't hate me.

Love,

Christine

I trace her signature, *Love, Christine*. She must have written this on her lap, the letters are carved into the paper and easy to feel. I shiver imagining the paper pressed to her thigh as she poured out her heart onto it. I can't lie. It's bittersweet, but, I suppose, fitting that our relationship should begin and end with a letter.

Yeah, she tried to add some hope there, but I know what this is. A very generously written break-up letter. Although, she's right, did we even have time to really call it a relationship? I guess not for her.

But I can't completely squash that kernel of hope. At the end of the day, she has decided to come with me. I wouldn't have chosen this for either of us. But she did. And I'm sure, that son of a bitch, Leo, spelled out all her options. And she did it anyway.

Even though the implied meaning of the letter hurts, I smile anyway. There's no denying, she's an amazing girl.

So, I guess there's nothing else for me to do right now. Just figure out how to get discharged from this place and head off into the sunset with Tweedle Dee and Tweedle Dum. Then, start the timer for three years and hope we can get on with life, together, then.

52

Christine

Daria was sitting in the living room when I brought Leo back to the apartment. She wore her rage on her face and lit into me as soon as I pushed open the remains of the smashed door.

"Here you are!" she exclaimed, fury mixed with relief. "You had me scared to death. Broken door. Blood all over the floor. No note. The police just left. I'll have to call them back and tell them you weren't abducted. It's almost a shame you're alive, because I'm going to kill you!"

"I'm sorry," I said. "I should have called you from the hospital."

"You think?" She turned to Leo, noticing him for the first time. "And who the hell are you?" she asked.

"Leo." He said, calm as ever. "I'm a friend of Gabriel's."

"Get out," Daria said, pointing to what was left of the door. "I'm not having anything to do with him, and that includes you. Out!"

Leo glanced at me and turned back to the door. "I'll wait in the car."

"No," I said to Daria. "Leo isn't—"

Daria shook her head. "I'm not covering for you anymore. This is too much for me. I called your parents. They're on their way."

The words stung, but not because it meant they'd bring me to Texas. That didn't matter anymore. Gabriel was gone. Tiffany was heading to France. Daria was through with me. There was nothing left in Michigan for me.

I looked down and caught sight of a bloodstain on the carpet. Which of us had left it?

"You did the right thing." I said. "I'm sorry about everything."

Daria rubbed her hands over her face, and when she looked at me again, there were tears in her eyes.

"I can't even imagine what you went through here," she cried. She came over and wrapped me in a trembling hug. "I'm so glad you're okay."

I hugged her tight, glad that she didn't hate me after all.

"I never meant for things to get so out of control. It isn't Gabriel's fault though."

"Hush," Daria chided. "I don't care about Gabriel. I just care about you."

I could live with that.

"I guess it's going to be awhile before I see you again," I said, knowing it would be even longer than she imagined.

Daria released me from the hug and regarded me with watery eyes.

"You'll be back," she said quietly.

I nodded, even though I doubted I ever would.

53

Christine

There were two and a half hours before my flight to Texas was scheduled to take off. Since no one besides Leo and me knew what had happened at Daria's apartment (and we weren't telling), we had described it as a random break and enter. I had explained Gabriel's disappearance by saying we'd broken up and that Leo and I were together. It wasn't a hard sell. My parents didn't know anything about Gabriel anyway. Their guilt had intensified one hundredfold when they heard I'd been the victim of a break in, and it wasn't hard to convince them that we shouldn't go to Texas until after Tiffany's party. It was a good thing Tiffany was having a going away party. It would have to serve as a farewell for both of us.

My parents hovered in the kitchen with Tiffany's parents while I sat in her living room with my friends for the last time.

Leo had excused himself for a bathroom break, giving Daria the opportunity to cut to the chase.

"I don't know why he was friends with Gabriel, but I like who you are with Leo. He's level. Like the old you."

I didn't know what to say. We weren't really to-gether. We'd just been through a lot together. I'd also learned how to bluff really well.

Tiffany giggled. "You do complement each other. Just like Marcel and me."

Marcel leaned over and kissed Tiffany's cheek, and Daria made a "gag me" face. I chuckled, so happy that I was leaving my friends on a good note.

Leo came back and sat beside me. He still looked rough from his injuries. It was actually surprising that Daria would give him the seal of approval with that bruised nose. He'd also been diagnosed with a mild concussion and bruised ribs. Of course, Leo did exude a calm, confident presence, even through all that. He talked easily with Daria and Javier. He'd even submit-ted willingly when Tiffany greeted him with a hug. If things had been different, we would have made a fun group.

All too soon, my parents appeared behind me and mom put her hands on my shoulders. "It's so nice to see you all together," she said in a waver-y voice. "But we need to head to the airport pretty soon."

I looked around at my friends. Tiffany had a re-signed smile on her face. Marcel smiled politely. Daria had a new version of the pity face. Leo looked like he was trying to transfer some confidence my way.

Javier was the one, the poetic soul, to capture the moment. He raised his can of Coke. "To following our individual paths to greatness."

The rest of us raised our drinks and clunked them together.

I didn't know if my new path would lead to greatness, but it was definitely my own path to follow. Everything had changed in one summer, just part of one summer, really. Tiffany was following Marcel to France. I was following Gabriel into the dreamworld, and who could say what I was following Leo into. Judging by the smile in his eyes as he looked at me, I was pretty sure it was going to be worth it to find out.

Acknowledgements

I'd like to extend my sincere thanks to the following people for their roles in making *Dream Girl* a reality.

Mom & Dad: You always encouraged my love of stories and never doubted that I would be an author. You laid the foundation for success. This one's for you.

Jeff: I could never have done this without all the times you wrangled the kids so I could steal some writing time. Thank you for supporting this crazy dream of mine. I love you.

Patty: You left your mark on this book even before you were born.

Ted: You made me realize if not now, when?

Michael Lawrence: Your *Aldous Lexicon* was the key I needed to unlock this book. Thank you, so much, for everything. More than you know.

Jody Lamb: Words can't express how grateful I am to have gone through this whole process with you. We were always so much closer than we thought, but Gordon Korman knew all along.

Dave Richards: Thanks for being the writing buddy I needed to get through that final stretch. For the root beer and Doritos we celebrated with in the break room. You're awesome.

To Mrs. Maggie Kelly: For not only reading drafts

and parts of drafts, but for being a brilliant proofreader. You're a super star.

To early readers of various versions, especially Paul McGlynn, Melissa Shanker and Meline Scheidel. You all helped to make this a better story. I hope you're proud of the final result.

John Bolton: I consider you my first "real" fan and, now, a friend. Your name is in print in my book. Time to get it on your own.

My wonderful (and numerous) aunts, uncles and cousins: Your support and enthusiasm means so much. And you, Steve Hornback, get a special shout-out because of your enthusiasm for *Kiss of Death*. Hope you like this one too.

Jennifer Karberg, Heather Murray and Samantha Harris for "Biosphere." Catherine Adams for the comedy sketches. Lisa Barrett for the poetry. Those were the days that solidified my love of writing. I'm so glad to have shared them with you.

Rich Chase: for every conversation we've ever had, and for your constant question, "When are you going to publish that book?"

Laura Fawcett: for taking me up on that contest, so long ago, which earned you a character named after you. I finally delivered!

Jennifer Baum: for reading this story and loving it enough to put it in print. You're a dream come true.

Mel Corrigan and the Scribe family of authors: I'm so happy to be part of such a great team.

About the Author

Photo Credit: The Memory Keeper Photography

S.J. Lomas lives in Southeastern Michigan with her husband, two children and a cat. Although she's never been to the dreamworld, this book was inspired by a dream. When she's not writing she likes to read, sing along to her favorite music and have fun with her family. You can keep up with S.J. on her website, www.sjlomas.com.

CPSIA information can be obtained at www.ICGtesting.com
Printed in the USA
LVOW13s1821171013

357416LV00001B/1/P